BEYOND THE OPEN DOOR

Other Apple Paperbacks
you will enjoy:

The Ghost in the Noonday Sun
by Sid Fleischman

Into the Dark
by Nicholas Wilde

Sleepers, Wake
by Paul Samuel Jacobs

The Adventures of Boone Barnaby
by Joe Cottonwood

The Lampfish of Twill
by Janet Taylor Lisle

BEYOND THE OPEN DOOR

Original title: *With My Knife*

Andrew Lansdown

AN
APPLE
PAPERBACK

SCHOLASTIC INC.
New York Toronto London Auckland Sydney

The author gratefully acknowledges the financial assistance of the Literature Board of the Australia Council for the writing of the first draft of *With My Knife*.

Originally published as *With My Knife*

ISBN 0-590-47160-0

12 11 10 9 8 7 6 5 4 3 2   5 6 7 8/9

Printed in the U.S.A.   40

First Scholastic printing, November 1993

CONTENTS

For my children
Stephen, Tamah and Naomi

Thou hast sore broken us in the place of dragons.
Psalm 44:19 (The Holy Bible, King James Version)

I THE KNIFE

COLYN was digging potatoes with his father when he found the knife. It was buried quite deep and a large potato had grown around the blade, as if someone had stabbed the knife right through it.

Colyn ran to his father, who was digging several rows nearer the river. "Look!" he shouted. "Look what I've found!"

His father took the knife. "Well, I'll be," he said, holding the knife by its blade to test its balance. "Do you know what, son? This was my knife once."

"Yours!" cried Colyn, surprised and disappointed.

"Yep. When I was a boy ... How old are you now?"

"You know, Dad! It's my birthday tomorrow."

"That's right." His father was remembering. "It was the day before my tenth birthday, too. I found it wedged in some rocks on the other side of the river. My father let me keep it. But on my birthday I chopped the edge of the kitchen table while I was waiting for Mum to put tea out. So Dad took it off me. He never gave it back."

"How do you know this is the one?" Colyn asked. But he knew the answer. The handle was wood, richly brown, like jarrah, and had a circle etched on one side and a tapering triangle on the other. The blade was long, thin and slightly crescent-shaped. No one could forget a knife like that.

"See how the blade looks like stone?" said his father.

The blade was almost black and had a dull sheen. There was not a spot of rust on it. And the handle was clean and smooth, as if it had been polished by constant use rather than lying lost in the soil for years.

"I s'pose *you'll* keep it now," said Colyn.

"Well, I'm not going to chuck it away," his father said, putting the knife into one of the deep pockets of his overalls.

Although he did not know it until that moment, Colyn had been wanting a knife of his own for a long time.

"What will you do with it?" he asked, trying not to sound sooky or mean.

His father had begun digging again. He glanced up at Colyn and suddenly he realised what his son was feeling. He thrust the shovel into the dark loam and propped his right foot on it.

"The trouble with a bloke rearing a son on his own," he said, "is he forgets that a boy is only little, and sort of tender. Now your mother, she was tender. And she would've kept an eye on me, to make sure I didn't forget."

Colyn could not remember his mother. She had died when he was barely three. He would be ten tomorrow, and he could not remember. Sometimes when his father spoke about her, his eyes would go distant and glassy, as if he were not behind them any more. But this time he blinked a bit and smiled at Colyn. He took the knife from his pocket and flicked the blade with his thumb.

"Finders keepers," he said.

Colyn's eyes widened. "I can keep it?"

"Provided you don't do anything silly like chopping the table."

"Oh, I promise!"

His father laughed and slapped Colyn on the back. "Here you are then," he said. "Mind you," he added, "it doesn't mean you can have a bludge. Still plenty of spuds in the ground."

That night, as he sat in the lounge-room by the fire with his father, Colyn began to carve a piece of wood. He had no idea what he wanted to make. He just started whittling. The knife was sharp and shaved the wood easily.

"You're making a mess," his father growled.

Colyn did not look up. "I'll sweep it after," he said.

Before long, Colyn realised that the wood had begun to take on a shape. But what? He stared at it intently, turning it around in his hands. It looked a bit like a dog. "Just what I've always wanted," Colyn murmured; and he began to try, with all his might, to carve a dog. But the harder he tried, the less like a dog the piece of wood became.

"Blow!"

His father looked up from the book he was reading. "What's the matter?"

Colyn passed him the carving. "I want to make a

dog," he said. "But it keeps going wrong."

"It's not easy to carve something." His father looked at the work carefully. "You have to be patient. Practice and patience, that's how most things are learnt." He handed it back. "Anyway," he said, "it's time for bed now, so you'll have to put it away."

"No," said Colyn. "I'll start a new one tomorrow." He threw the carving into the fire. As it landed on the coals, he thought he heard a dog bark way off in the distance.

When Colyn woke, it was his birthday. But the first thing he thought of was his knife. He reached under his pillow, and there it was, just as he had left it last night, just as he had dreamed.

His father came into his room with two presents and sat on his bed. "Be careful with that knife. It's sharp."

"It's not sharp for me," said Colyn, "only everything else."

"Well, why don't you put it down for a minute and have a look at what I've got you?"

Colyn unwrapped his presents. One was a thousand-piece jigsaw puzzle, the other a leather football.

"One for your brain and one for your body," his father laughed.

Because it was his birthday, Colyn did not have to work. After breakfast he kicked his football along the gravel road in front of the potato paddock. But he had no one to kick it back to him, so he soon grew tired of it. He thought of his friends at school and wished, briefly, that the term holidays were ending rather than beginning. He left the ball by the road and wandered across the paddock. The loam was dry and soft, and little puffs of dust burst from beneath his boots as he walked.

There was a place along the river where a tree had fallen into the water. It was Colyn's special place. He climbed on to the trunk and walked out to where it sank beneath the surface. He sat down and stared at the water eddying past. In the backwater of the log a swarm of water-beetles swirled crazily about each other. A blue dragonfly hovered over them.

Colyn jabbed his knife into the trunk absent-mindedly, prised off a lump of bark, and flicked it into the water. While watching the bark bob away on the current, he decided to carve his name.

He spent nearly an hour carving his name carefully and deeply. He felt so pleased with it when he had finished that he thought to carve his father's name too. But after finishing the first letter he said out loud, as if talking to someone, "It's not working. He should have carved his own name when he owned it. But it's my knife now."

After a while he felt lonely, so he wandered over to see his father.

"How's it going, son?"

Colyn shrugged. "Nothing to do," he said.

"Plenty of spuds to dig and bag."

"But it's my birthday," Colyn protested, sitting down beside the sack his father was filling with newly-dug potatoes.

He took a small potato from the sack and began to peel it. He had never peeled one with a knife before, and he was surprised at how well he could do it. The potato seemed to shed its skin as the knife touched it. As the last patch of skin fell off, leaving it perfectly white, the potato seemed to change. Colyn weighed it in his hand. It felt heavier. He bit it. It was hard, like a stone!

"Look at this potato, Dad."

His father took the stone from him. "Yes," he said, "it does look like a potato, a peeled one."

"It *is* a potato," said Colyn. "I peeled it with my knife and it turned into a stone."

"Go on, you scallywag!" His father laughed, ruffling his hair.

"But it's true!" Colyn insisted. "I'll show you."

He took another potato and began to peel it while his father looked on. But this time the peel did not come away easily. When he had finished, he held it in his open palm, staring at it, but it did not change into a stone.

"I suppose you'll be telling me that you can turn stones into potatoes next," smiled his father. "Think of all the stones in the riverbed. All we'd have to do is wait till summer when the river dries and then pick them up!"

His father unearthed several large potatoes. Colyn took one and walked back towards the river.

He sat on the fallen tree beside his carved name and set to work with his knife. As the last bit of peel fell away, the potato became heavy and hard in his hand. He bit it and it hurt his teeth. He banged the log and it bruised the wood.

"See, I wasn't imagining!" he said.

COLYN was washing the dishes. The window over the sink looked like a blackboard. There might have been stars in the sky outside but the kitchen light stopped him from seeing them. The knife was in his belt and when he leaned against the sink cupboard the handle pressed into his stomach.

Because his thoughts were racing his hands were dawdling. Without looking at it, he had been slowly rubbing the frying-pan for several minutes.

"That might work!" he exclaimed.

He quite forgot the dirty plates in his excitement. He rummaged in the cupboard for the biggest potato he could find. After washing it, he cut a thin slice from it. The flesh was firm and white.

"Come and I'll show you something, Dad."

His father had just settled himself by the fire. "Can't it wait?"

"Aw, come on, Dad!" he said. "You'll really like it."

His father looked up and saw Colyn holding the knife and the slice of potato. He sighed, but he got up from his chair without further badgering and followed

7

Colyn outside.

There was no moon so the stars were intensely bright.

"Now watch this," Colyn said, and he flung the round slice of potato high into the air. It fell to the ground about five metres away. They could just see it faintly reflecting the sparse starlight.

"It didn't work!" Colyn shouted angrily.

"What did you expect it to do?" asked his father.

"I don't know," Colyn said, kicking the dirt.

After his father had gone back inside the house, Colyn picked up the potato slice. He turned it over in his hands, wondering what to do with it. He held it by the edge, brought it back to his chest, then flung it like a frisbee. It fell to the ground again and broke in half. He left it there and returned to the kitchen.

The dishwater was cold. He let it out and filled the sink from the kettle.

After he had finished the dishes, he sat with his father by the fire and stared into the flames. Two blocks of jarrah were burning quite quickly, but a large mallee root seemed untouched by the flames, except for several knobs that glowed redly. After a while he reached into the wood-box, chose a small lump of wood, and began to carve it. Although jarrah is a hard wood, the knife cut through it easily. It was like carving soap.

Colyn concentrated intently. He wanted to make a dog. But again he had no success. The harder he tried, the less like a dog the piece of wood became.

"Why don't you try the jigsaw puzzle?" suggested his father when he saw that Colyn was becoming upset. "I'll help you."

"I can't yet," said Colyn, almost crying. "I have to make a dog."

At bedtime he threw the carving into the fire. It burned without a sound.

The next day, while he was digging potatoes with his father, Colyn's thoughts wandered back over last night's failure. When he threw the potato disc, what did he expect to happen? And why didn't it? He pondered these questions over and again.

"Come on," his father said the first time Colyn stopped work. "Daydreaming doesn't get the work done."

The next time Colyn stopped work, his father said, "What's up, son?"

"Nothing," Colyn said. He picked up a potato, stared at it, then dropped it into the bag. He touched the knife, which he wore in his belt.

The third time Colyn stopped work, his father looked at him for a moment, and then he looked towards the river where Colyn was staring. "Boy," he said, "you might as well go and play. I'll call you when I want you."

Colyn strolled down to the river. The water was ruffled by the breeze and dappled with shade. A duck flew off and a dabchick dived as he approached. He looked where he had carved his name in the fallen tree. He sat down and ran his fingers along the grooves of the letters. His fingers felt his name: COLYN LARKIN. He closed his eyes and imagined he was a blind boy reading a special name.

"Colyn!"

He opened his eyes with a start. "What?" he said,

looking about.

"Time for lunch," his father called from the riverbank.

"But I only just got here."

"You've been gone for two hours," his father said. "You must've fallen asleep. Lucky you didn't fall in the water!"

After washing the dishes that night, Colyn peeled a small potato with his knife. It became a stone.

He found a large potato and cut a slice from it. It did not change into stone. He put the slice on the table and thought for a moment.

"Perhaps it's the peel," he murmured.

He picked up the slice again and began to cut the peel carefully from its edge. As the skin came off like a thin brown ribbon and fell to the floor, the potato slice turned to stone.

Colyn wiped the blade of his knife on his pants and then poked it into his belt. Still holding the potato-disc, he picked up the small potato-stone and ran outside.

He threw the potato-stone into the air. It sped off like a shooting star, only it shot up to the heavens instead of down to the earth. He watched it streak away until it disappeared. Then he hurled the potato-disc into the air. It began to glow as it left his hand. It flew up and up, glowing brighter as it rose higher, until it hovered in the black sky like a full moon.

Colyn stared in amazement. "A moon!" he said softly, as if saying it could help him believe what he had done. He stood entranced for several minutes before running into the house.

"Quick, Dad!" he shouted. "Come and look at the moon!"

He ran outside, then darted back to make sure his father was following. But by the time his father joined him the disc had faded.

His father looked up. "There's no moon out tonight, son," he said.

Colyn shook his head and looked up. "But I made one."

"What? A moon?"

"Yes," said Colyn. "I made one. With my knife."

"Oh Colyn!" His father sounded annoyed. "What's got into you lately?"

"I *did*!" Colyn protested. "I *did* make one! I cut the potato like last night and I threw it up and it became a moon!"

His father shook his head. "You'd better come in now," he said. "It's cold."

Oₙ Sunday neither Colyn nor his father worked in the potato paddock.

"What're you going to do today?" asked his father.

"I don't know," said Colyn.

"We could try that jigsaw puzzle," his father suggested.

Colyn did not really feel like piecing together a jigsaw, but he did not feel like doing anything else either. "All right," he said.

"You get the box and I'll clear the table," his father said.

On the jigsaw box there was a picture of a dragon. It was a bluish-grey colour and had orange flames shooting from its nostrils. It was flying and its wings blotted out the sky. Colyn tipped the pieces on to the table.

Colyn's father pulled up a chair and began to sort through the jumble, looking for the pieces with a straight edge.

"The easiest way is to make the border first," he said.

Colyn began to look for straight-edged pieces too. "Here's a corner," he said.

"Good," said his father. "Keep it to one side. That'll be our starting piece." He was quiet for a few seconds, then he said, "You know, Colyn, your mother and I used to do jigsaw puzzles together. I remember one in particular. It had over four thousand pieces and took us a fortnight to finish. It was a picture of a battle between some funny-looking dragons and men on horses. Your mother was carrying you then. I remember because her tummy was big and she kept bumping the table and knocking pieces on to the floor."

"Did you feel me when I was in her tummy?"

"Yes. You used to punch and kick like a Chinese boxer!"

"Did I hurt her?"

"No." His father laughed. "She said you made her feel uncomfortable at times, but you never hurt her."

"I wish she was here," said Colyn.

"So do I," said his father, squeezing Colyn's shoulder. "She would have liked doing a jigsaw with you. Especially one of a dragon."

Colyn's father found another corner piece and put it aside.

"There's a verse about dragons in the Bible," he said. "Your mother used to recite it to herself sometimes. She'd go dreamy and she'd say it." He stood up suddenly, pushing the chair back with his legs. "She had it marked. Hang on a tick and I'll find it."

He left the room briskly and came back within a few moments.

"Here," he said, opening the old Bible and moistening his finger to flip the thin pages. "Here it is, in

Psalm forty-four: 'Thou hast sore broken us in the place of dragons.' Only she used to say, 'You have sore broken *me* in the place of dragons.' She thought it was the most beautiful and lonely thing."

Colyn took the Bible and read the whole verse. *Thou hast sore broken us in the place of dragons, and covered us with the shadow of death.* He looked at his father thoughtfully. "Are dragons real?" he asked.

"No, I don't think so."

"Then how can we have pictures of them?"

"People imagine them," his father said. "It doesn't mean they're real."

"Did Mum believe in them?"

Colyn's father looked serious suddenly. "Son," he said, shaking his head, "you teach me new things about your mother every day. Yes, I think she did. I think she did believe in them and it made her sad." Then, as if he had said something foolish, he laughed and said, "Come on! Let's get to this puzzle."

After they had found all the edge pieces, they began to fit them together. By mid-morning they had pieced the entire border together. They had a square with a smooth edge on the outside and a wobbly edge on the inside. Within the square the brown table-top waited to be covered with the picture of the dragon.

"I'm going to make a cup of tea," Colyn's father said. "Do you want a drink of hot chocolate?"

"No," said Colyn. "I want to go to the river. Can I?"

His father looked at the puzzle and then at his son. "Yes, I suppose so," he said. "We can finish it later."

As he crossed the paddock, Colyn found a large

potato and a knobbly piece of wood. He took them with him to his special place by the river.

A grey heron flew up, croaking, as he scrambled down the bank. A pair of black ducks whacked the water with their wings and sped off with a whistling sound.

Colyn climbed on to the fallen tree trunk. As he stepped over his name, he noticed the first and only letter he had carved of his father's name. For some reason it made him sad. "If only he hadn't lost the knife when he was a boy like me," he said softly.

He took out his knife and looked at it. He touched the tip of the blade with his finger, pressing down on it until he could feel that it was about to pierce him. He lifted his finger off the point and looked at the mark in his skin.

"My knife," he said.

He picked up the piece of wood he had found and examined it, turning it over in his hands. What would be the best way to carve it to make a dog come out? He imagined that the two twiggy bits at one end could be the front legs of a running dog. He set to work with his knife to make them into a dog's legs. He worked carefully and finally he succeeded. He had carved two perfect legs reaching out from the wood. He was excited.

"Now for the head," he said.

But the head did not work out well. He gouged too deeply for one eye and he slipped while carving an ear and cut it right off.

"I hate you!" he said to the wood, and he threw it into the river.

For just a moment, when the wood hit the water, Colyn thought he saw the carved front legs of the almost-dog splashing about as if it were trying to swim. He blinked and looked again. There was no movement. It was just a piece of wood floating away.

Colyn stabbed the knife into the log. It wobbled in the wood as he let it go. He sat on the log, dangling his feet into the water and feeling the breeze in his hair. He watched the reflected sunlight dance in small pieces on the shaggy trunks of the paperbark trees. A spider ran across the water by his leg.

He felt lazy and happy. He looked at his knife and admired its gleaming black blade and its polished brown handle with the triangle carved on the side facing him. He plucked the knife from the log and rubbed the triangle with his finger.

"I wonder," he said.

He picked up the potato and cut a slice from it. He cut a triangle in the centre of the slice, then peeled it. It turned to stone—a flat, circular stone with a triangular window in it.

He held the window to his eye and looked through it at a large rock on the far bank. The rock was not there. Instead he saw a white, swirling mist. He took the window-stone away and the rock reappeared. He looked through the window again and the rock was gone.

His heart was beating quickly. He put his finger through the window. His finger disappeared. He could see it going in but not coming out.

He withdrew his finger and put the blade of his knife through the window. The blade did not disappear. He could see it going in and passing through and coming out. He touched the tip of the blade and it cut his finger. He wiped the blood on his handkerchief.

He raised the window-stone to his eye again. He looked at the trees but saw a white mist. He looked at the blue sky and saw only whiteness. He looked at the water and saw ... He saw the swirling whiteness but there was something else. What? He looked intently. It came into focus. It was an eye, an eye with a slit pupil, a large yellow eye staring back at him.

Colyn screamed and dropped the window-stone. It fell spinning into the water as he scrambled to his feet and began to run.

By the time he reached home, he was not feeling so frightened. He took a deep breath and stepped into the house.

"You weren't long," said his father, looking up from the newspaper. Then he noticed Colyn's finger. "You've cut yourself," he said. "If you aren't more careful with that knife I'll have to put it away until you're older."

"Oh, no!" cried Colyn, clutching at the handle above his belt.

His father looked surprised. "I'm not going to take it, son," he said. "I'm just telling you to be careful with it."

"I will!" said Colyn earnestly. "It was just an accident. It's my knife. It won't cut me again."

"Well, let's get a bandaid on that finger," his father said. "Then we can get back to the puzzle."

Colyn and his father worked on the jigsaw well into the afternoon. Piece by piece, the dragon took shape.

"Lucky last," said his father, handing Colyn the last

piece of the puzzle. "You put it in."

Colyn snapped the piece in place. It completed the dragon's yellow eye.

Colyn turned pale and began to tremble. He put his hand to his knife, as if to steady himself.

His father reached out to him. "What's the matter, Colyn?" he said. His voice was urgent and troubled.

Colyn hugged his father. "The dragon's eye," he said, hugging his father tighter than ever. "I've seen the dragon's eye."

IV THE CARVING

COLYN sat by the fire, absent-mindedly whittling a piece of wood. His hands seemed to work by themselves as he thought back over the day's events. The flat circular stone with the triangular window; the mist through the triangle; the jigsaw puzzle; the dragon's eye. What did these things mean?

His father's voice interrupted his thoughts. "Well, if that isn't the best carving I've seen in my life!"

Colyn looked at the piece of wood in his hand. He gasped. It had been transformed into the most exquisite carving of a kelpie dog.

Its legs were finely tufted with fur and its tail was long and flowing. Its head was cocked to one side. One ear stood up and the other flopped down. Its mouth was slightly open as if it were panting, revealing its teeth and tongue, and it seemed to be actually *looking* at them from its tiny, perfect eyes.

"I did it!" Colyn said finally. "I did it like I always wanted!"

"Yes," said his father. "You certainly did." He took the carving from Colyn and looked at it closely. He ran

...is fingers over the dog's lean body and down along its flowing tail. He felt its ears and eyes and nose. "Strike!" he said. "Its nose feels damp! Except that it's so small, it could almost be real."

He handed it back to Colyn, who placed it in his lap. Colyn stroked it lovingly, and his father reached out to touch it from time to time, too. The carved dog seemed to be watching them. The fire burnt down and became a rubble of red coals.

"Good heavens!" said his father. "Look at the time! You should've been in bed an hour ago."

That night Colyn was troubled by dreams. He dreamed that his carved dog was gone, stolen. He dreamed that he was searching for it in the white mists. In his sleep, he reached under the pillow to hold his knife. With his other arm he reached down to the floor beside his bed and held a shoe that he dreamed was his dog. He held his knife and he held the shoe through the night, through the dreams that made him sweat and cry. When he woke, he was still holding them.

He woke suddenly, as if someone had called his name. It was early morning. Pale light was shining into his room around the edges of the blind. He looked at his knife and smiled. He looked at the shoe and dropped it as if it were a burning coal. He leaned over the bed to find the dog. It was not there. He threw off the blankets and knelt on the floor to look under his bed. He searched about his room frantically, but the dog was gone.

"Dad!" he yelled, running into his father's bedroom. "Dad!" He shook him awake.

His father was confused at first, then angry. "No, I didn't take it," he snapped. "Why would I want to take it? Now go back to bed and let me sleep a bit longer. If you bother me again I'll crown you."

Colyn ran back to his room and had another look.. It was no use. The carved dog was gone. He dressed quietly and stole outside, holding his knife.

It was cold out. His breath was like smoke. There was frost on the grass. The sun was standing among the trees and its light was low and soft. A magpie carolled sweetly and tiny birds were twittering. Colyn felt terribly alone.

He walked to the packing shed, a big shed made of corrugated iron and a raised concrete floor. He climbed up and looked around at the sacks of potatoes and farm equipment. A spider made a St Andrew's cross in a web in an old harness hanging on a nail. A rat ran along a rafter. A willie wagtail landed on the floor in the doorway, casting a long, nervous shadow on the concrete.

Colyn opened a sack and chose a large potato. He cut a slice from it, cut a triangle in the slice, then peeled it.

He lifted the window-stone to his eye and peered through it. He looked at the sacks and they became mist. He looked at the spider and it swirled away. He looked at his legs and they were gone. He looked and looked but saw nothing but whiteness.

Finally, he held up his knife and looked at it through the triangular window. The blade did not disappear, but shone black and sharp. His hand was not there, nor was the knife-handle, which was mostly hidden in his hidden

...and. But the knife-blade remained entire, floating alone in space with the white mist boiling about it.

It was then that he heard a sound that seemed to come from a far corner of the shed. He looked around and was about to investigate when he heard his father call.

Colyn put the window-stone in his pocket and walked to the shed doorway. "I'm here!" he called.

His father stepped down from the veranda of the house and strode towards him.

Colyn heard the noise again: a scratching, rustling noise, like someone poking about at the back of the shed. He turned in time to see a small dog scamper from the shadows.

The boy held his breath as the dog trotted to his side, sniffed his right leg, woofed twice, then sat down and began to thump the concrete floor with his tail.

Colyn blinked in disbelief. "Oh," he said. "There you are. You're alive." The dog looked up at him, his head cocked to the side, one ear pricked, the other bent.

His father reached the shed. "Hello," he said. "Where'd the mutt come from?"

Colyn knelt to pat the kelpie. "I made him," he said. "With my knife."

V   THE DOG

COLYN could not swallow his toast, he was so excited. He could not sit still, either. He sat in his chair and then he stood up and then he plopped down again.

The dog sat by the stove, looking at Colyn earnestly with his head cocked and his mouth partly open. He was completely brown, except for one ear—the ear that stood up like a small, sharp triangle—which was white. He never took his eyes off Colyn and he thumped his tail on the floor every time the boy stood up.

The dog was bigger than Colyn's carving but otherwise he looked exactly the same.

"Oh, Dad!" Colyn said. "Isn't he lovely!"

His father nodded.

"I can keep him, can't I, Dad?"

"Yes," his father said. "Yes, but you mustn't pat him during meals and he's not to get on to your bed. And you have to look after him and feed him and keep him clean. I've got enough to keep me busy without a dog to be bothered with."

"I'll look after him," Colyn said. "That's just what I

want to do." He stood up again. "My own dog!" he said. He felt his knife in his belt. "I can make anything with my knife!"

His father looked at him seriously. "I know you're left to yourself a lot, son," he said, "but you have to be careful about the things you imagine. You've got to remember that some things are real and some are only pretending, and you've got to remember which ones are which. Otherwise you'll end up in strife further down the track. Anyway," he added cheerfully, "now you've got a dog to keep you company, maybe you'll stick in the real world."

Throughout the morning Colyn worked hard with his father. The dog was always by his side and he patted him from time to time but he never stopped work. He dug one row of potatoes while his father dug another. By lunchtime his father was only a little way ahead.

Colyn gobbled the sandwiches his father had made and gulped the raspberry cordial. "Can I go now?" he asked.

His father looked at the dog. "Be back in an hour," he said.

"Yippee!" Colyn yelled, and he raced towards the river with his dog yapping at his heels.

The dog ran on to the tree trunk ahead of him. He sniffed at the letters of Colyn's name, then stepped over them and trotted to the place where the trunk sank beneath the river. He lapped some water before returning to lie down by the name.

Colyn stepped over him and sat down. "I'll show you something," he said.

He withdrew his knife from his belt and reached for the half-potato he had left on the log the day before. He cut a slice and peeled it so that it turned to stone. Holding the stone disc with his forefinger curved around its edge, he bent towards the water and took aim. The dog looked at him quizzically.

"Now watch this," Colyn said.

He threw the disc sideways along the river so that it hit the water flat-on and skipped across the smooth surface. Because of the sunlight, Colyn did not notice the disc glow as it glided away. It skimmed down the river like a swallow, leaving rings of ripples where it touched the water with the tip of its wing. On and on it skipped until it came to a bend in the river, where it took a last leap and buried itself in the bank.

Colyn cut two more slices and skipped them along. They sped away from his hand, seeming to gather speed with every bounce. One hit a flooded gum at the bend in the river and stuck in the trunk.

Colyn had used up the potato. "I should have brought a couple with me," he said. The dog licked his hand.

"I know," Colyn said. He reached into his pocket and took out the window-stone he had made that morning. The dog sat up and pricked his ears.

Colyn laughed. "Watch this," he said.

He poked his finger through the triangular window and it disappeared. The dog growled.

"Look," said Colyn, pulling his finger out. "See? Back again."

He lifted the stone to his eye. He looked through the window to see the whiteness. The dog growled again.

"What's the matter?" Colyn said. "Do you want to have a look?"

He put the stone to the dog's right eye. The dog jumped to his feet and backed away, bristling and snarling. He bared his teeth fiercely.

"All right, silly," said Colyn. "You don't have to look."

He raised the stone to his own eye again and looked at the dog. What he saw made him gasp. For an instant he saw, or thought he saw, the dog running away through the mist. Then there was nothing but the swirling whiteness. He heard the dog snarling faintly, as if he were far away.

Colyn felt suddenly afraid. He took the stone from his eye. The dog was no longer standing on the log. He was gone.

"Oh!" Colyn cried, tears stinging his eyes. "Oh, please! Please come back!"

The dog woofed. Colyn glanced up to see him on the bank. He scampered back on to the log, wagging his tail. Colyn hugged him, crying into his fur.

"I thought you'd gone," he said.

The dog whined and licked his face.

After he had recovered from his fright, Colyn thought of the window-stone in his hand. He looked at it and sighed.

"I can make another one," he said. And he threw it low along the river. With each skip, a spurt of water shot up from the triangular hole. At the river's bend the stone hit the tree that had been struck earlier and cut right through it. It fell forward with a great crash into the water.

The dog barked furiously. Colyn's father came running. He stopped on the bank above Colyn's special place.

"You all right, son?" he called.

Colyn looked up. "Yeah," he said. "It was just a tree falling down." He pointed to where the tree lay half submerged in the water.

His father scrambled down the bank to join him. "Odd," he said. "There's not a breath of wind. It must've been rotten or something."

He bent down to pat the dog. "Give you a bit of a start, did it, pooch?" he said, scratching him under his chin. He looked at Colyn. "What're you going to call the little bloke, anyway?" he asked.

"I don't know," said Colyn. "I think he's already got a name. Something special. I just have to find it."

VI. THE DOORWAY

COLYN always finished work early in the afternoons so that he could play for an hour or two before tea. On Friday his father let him go extra early. He was about to run off when he had an idea.

"You know that big box in the shed?" he said.

"The cardboard one the freezer came in?" his father said without looking up from the sack he was tying.

"Yes," Colyn replied. "Can I have it?"

"What for?"

"I just want to cut it up with my knife to make a cubby," Colyn said.

His father scowled at him.

"Please can I have it, Dad? We don't need it for anything."

His father sighed. "Well, I don't want a mess left about. So if you wreck it, make sure you chuck it on the rubbish heap for burning."

Colyn gave his father a hug. "Thanks, Dad," he said. He ran to the shed with the dog at his heels.

As soon as they entered the shed, the dog began to sniff about. He trotted under some machinery and then

28

scampered over some sacks. He darted behind an old cupboard and began to yap. There was a scuffling sound. The dog barked, and something squealed like a piglet.

"Good boy!" Colyn said as the dog trotted to him and laid a dead rat at his feet. He rubbed the dog's ears. "Dad'll like you for that!"

He kicked the rat through the doorway into the yard, then dragged the cardboard box from the back of the shed and set it in a clear space in the middle of the floor. It was a big box, taller than Colyn and about as wide as his outstretched arms. He found a broom and brushed the dust from its sides, then closed the flaps on the opening side and sealed them with his father's masking tape.

He looked at the box with satisfaction. It was large, clean and closed. Inside, with the air and the blackness, there was easily room for a ten-year-old boy.

Colyn took his knife from his belt. He walked around the box, chose the best side, then reached up and stabbed the knife through the cardboard. He dragged the blade down in a straight line. It cut easily. He made another cut, then a third.

As the third cut joined the second, a large piece of cardboard fell into the box. Colyn grabbed it by a corner, pulled it out and dropped it on the floor. He stood back to admire his handiwork.

He had cut a doorway in the shape of a large triangle. It was as tall as he was and quite a bit wider, except for the top where the triangle tapered to a point. He could step through it easily. And before he knew what he was doing, he did precisely that. He stepped into the box through the triangular doorway he had cut with his knife.

Immediately, he was wrapped in mist.

Fear gripped him. His heart began to race.

He spun around to step back through the doorway, back into the world where the sun shone into his father's shed. But that world was gone. The doorway was gone. He groped for it but could not find it. There was only the mist, white and damp and cold. He cried out in horror. Already he had lost all sense of direction. Then, stupidly, he began to run, outpacing his heart. Within seconds he tripped and fell. The fall brought him to his senses. He got up and stood still.

Something moved beside him. He looked up. A yellow eye—as large as a man's head and as bright as a gas lamp—stared down at him. He scrambled to his feet and reached for his knife. He held the weapon with both hands in front of his chest like a samurai swordsman. The blade gleamed blackly, threateningly. The eye blinked, then brightened fiercely. The creature it belonged to roared. The roar seemed to blow the mist away for a moment and Colyn caught a glimpse of a great wing, like a bat's, only immensely larger, as large as a circus tent.

In the silence after the roar, Colyn heard his dog bark. He turned towards the sound and ran. The dog was barking frantically. Suddenly, at the source of the sound, Colyn saw another eye. He faltered for a moment, uncertain where to run. He was cut off. Then the second eye vanished. The dog kept barking. Colyn began to run again. He was blind in the mist but he ran with all his might, without a thought of banging into anything. Suddenly his foot struck something and he tripped and fell through the doorway into the shed.

He lay on the concrete floor, gripping his knife and trembling. The dog whined and licked his face. Colyn hugged him tightly, burying his face in his warm fur.

The colour had returned to his face and he was no longer shaking by the time his father strolled into the shed with his hands in his overall pockets.

"Hello," his father said. He nodded at the box. "You've done it." He poked his head through the triangular doorway.

Colyn gasped.

"A cubby, hey?" his father said, putting his right foot through the doorway.

"Don't!" Colyn cried. He grabbed at his father's shirt.

But it was too late. His father stepped in and squatted down. "A bit cramped," he said, his voice sounding far away and hollow. He climbed out and straightened his shoulders, then stood back and looked at the doorway. "You know what you should've done?" he said. "You should've cut the opening along only two sides. That way the third side could've been a hinge and the flap could've been the door. Anyway," he continued, looking around the floor, "where's the bit you cut out? You could probably stick it on with masking tape and make a door that way."

Colyn searched around the box and beneath the workbench. The large piece of cardboard he had cut from the box was missing.

"I don't know where it is," he said. "I left it

right here."

As he said this, something occurred to him that made his skin prickle. He shuddered. When he had cut a triangular doorway he had also cut a triangular door. He had made two triangles. One was an opening, the other a closing. And the closing one was gone.

He ran his thumbnail along the lines of the triangle etched on the handle of his knife. The dog pricked up his ears and stared at him.

"I've lost the door," he said to himself. And he remembered the second eye he had seen in the mists.

VII THE INVADERS

COLYN was fast asleep and the dog was napping on a mat beside his bed. It was after midnight. Colyn's father was in bed and the house was in darkness.

Something disturbed the dog. He cocked his ears, raised his head and whined. He propped his paws on Colyn's pillow and licked his face. Colyn brushed him aside in his sleep. The dog pawed at his face, scratching him.

Colyn woke up, instinctively reaching under his pillow for his knife. He sat up, blinking in the blackness.

"What is it, boy?"

The dog whined. Colyn gripped his knife tightly. He sensed it too. Something was not right. It was night-time and yet there seemed to be a darkness over the house—a blackness deeper than the night itself. Then it passed.

Colyn got out of bed and dressed quickly. He tiptoed to the window and drew the curtains back. Suddenly, there it was again—a deep darkness. He looked up. A group of stars disappeared and then reappeared, as if a thundercloud had passed over them.

Colyn hurried to the kitchen and, without turning on the light, chose six potatoes from the cupboard—one large and five small ones. He peeled the five small ones so that they turned into stones. He cut four slices from the large potato and peeled them so that they turned into discs of stone.

All the time the blackness kept passing back and forth over the house.

Colyn wiped his knife and put it in his belt. He stowed the five stones in his pockets. Picking up the four discs, he crept outside.

The blackness passed over the house again, blotting out the stars. Colyn squinted, trying to see what it was, but could not make it out. There was no moon and the stars were too faint.

He took one of his discs and flung it into the sky. It spun up and up, gathering brightness, until it sat in the night sky like a full moon. It shone whitely, and by its light Colyn saw the dragon.

It was a huge creature. Each of its wings was larger than the house. Its neck and tail looked like rivers, snaking out from a slightly broader body. The beast was pitch black but the moon's light gleamed on its wings and body in much the same way as light shimmers on water at night.

The dragon was caught by surprise by Colyn's moon. It wheeled away abruptly, then bellowed like a bull and charged at it. Fire flared from its nostrils and the moon blackened and broke up.

Colyn threw up another moon. The dragon roared and

flew at it furiously. It snatched it in one of its great talons and crushed it to pieces.

Colyn threw up his last two discs, one after the other. The dragon seemed confused for a moment. It started towards one, then changed its mind and wheeled away towards the other. It destroyed the third moon easily.

The dragon was about to attack the fourth moon when the dog barked. It turned its great head and peered down. For the first time Colyn noticed its yellow eyes. It roared and flapped up into the night sky. Up and up it flew until Colyn could barely guess where it was between the stars.

The dog pranced around, barking. He stood on his hind legs and pawed the air, as if trying to climb into the black sky. Colyn knelt to pat him.

"Ssssh, boy!" he said. "You'll make it angry."

As he said this, he heard a faint whistling, roaring sound. He looked up and saw the darkness that was the dragon diving towards the earth. He watched in panic as it grew rapidly larger and larger. The dog barked madly, leaping up almost as high as Colyn's head.

Without taking his eyes off the dragon, Colyn reached into his pocket and withdrew one of the stones he had made with his knife. He weighed it in his hand as the beast continued to free-fall, wings folded, like a huge hawk.

As the dragon hurtled towards him, Colyn took aim and hurled the stone at its head. The dragon screamed and swerved to one side. The stone sped past it and into the heavens.

The force of its dive broken, the dragon began to

fly away from the earth once more to gain height for its next attack.

Colyn saw his chance. He threw another stone with all his might. It whistled past the dragon, forcing it to duck its head. He threw a third stone and this time the missile hit its target. There was a loud crack as the stone struck the base of the dragon's wing, snapping the bone. The dragon screamed, like a horse when it is frightened, and began to tumble from the sky. It tumbled over and over, its massive wings flaring like black sails. As it fell it screamed in terror, and with each scream flame shot from its nostrils. In the turmoil the flame struck its broken wing, which caught fire. Soon the whole dragon was burning as it plummeted towards the earth.

As if in a trance, Colyn watched the dragon fall. It disappeared from sight behind the trees that lined the river. There was an explosion as it hit the water, followed by a loud hissing sound.

Colyn's shoulders slumped. It was over. He had defeated the dragon.

He sat down, exhausted. "We did it, boy," he said.

But the dog began to growl. He stared towards the shed. His ears and tail stood up as if they had been starched.

Colyn looked towards the shed. "What's the matter?" he said, getting to his feet.

The dog raced off, barking. Colyn ran after him. The moon he had made shone brightly, lighting up the yard with its silvery light. Everything glistened and cast long shadows. His own shadow strode out before him like a lanky giant.

The dog reached the shed well before his master and scampered in. Colyn could hear him snapping and snarling.

Colyn was panting by the time he reached the shed, but what he saw did not allow him any time to catch his breath.

A dragon was sliding through the doorway that Colyn had cut in the cardboard box. Its head and a few metres of its scaly neck were poking out of the triangular space. Colyn could just see the tips of its wings, which were folded up like umbrellas. It was lying along the floor like an enormous snake, looking at the barking dog.

When Colyn entered the shed, the dragon reared up. It glared at him with its yellow, slit-pupilled eyes. The boy froze. The dragon blinked. Its forked tongue flicked in and out several times.

Colyn drew his knife from his belt. The dragon shook its head and roared. Colyn hesitated for a moment, then stepped slowly towards it with his knife clenched in his right hand, held out in front of his chest.

The dragon dropped its head to the floor and began to retreat. It slid backwards slowly, as if someone were reeling it in. Its scales scraped loudly and sounded like the links of a heavy chain being dragged across the concrete.

Colyn approached at the same pace as the dragon retreated until the beast disappeared back through the triangular doorway. The dog stopped barking, ran to the box and sniffed about.

Colyn sat down, facing the doorway. The dog trotted over and sat down beside him. He swapped the knife to his left hand and patted the dog with his right.

"I think we'd better stay here and keep guard," he said.

VIII THE KILL

THE sunlight streaming through the doorway of the shed woke Colyn. He sat up. He was stiff from sleeping curled up on the cold, hard floor. He stretched, blinked and looked around, confused. He gazed at the box. The dog was dozing peacefully in front of the triangular doorway, his head on his paws.

Suddenly Colyn remembered why he was not snuggled in his bed. He began to pant with panic. He saw a flaming dragon falling through the night sky and another dragon slithering into the shed.

He looked about anxiously. But everything was fine. He was in the real world, the world he knew and loved. The sun was shining. A swallow flitted through the rafters. There were no dragons here. He was safe.

He became aware of a pain in his left forearm, and saw that he was still clenching his knife. His knuckles were white. He felt his arm. The muscles were knotted tightly. He tried to let go of the knife but his fingers would not open. He stroked his arm to relieve the pain and relax the muscles.

While he was rubbing his arm, Colyn looked out

of the shed, across the gravel road, across the potato paddock, towards the gum trees that grew along the edge of the river.

"That's where the dragon fell," he said.

The dog pricked his ears and opened his eyes. He looked up at Colyn without moving his head.

"Come on, boy," Colyn said, patting his thigh. "Let's go and see."

The dog sneezed and stood up. He stretched and whined, then followed Colyn into the open.

The sun was tangled in the branches of the trees behind the shed. The colours were soft and the shadows were long. Colyn listened to the scrunch of his boots and the scratch of his dog's paws as they crossed the gravel road. He climbed through the fence into the potato paddock and began to run, leaping the rows of potatoes as if they were hurdles. The dog kept pace with him.

They scrambled down the riverbank at Colyn's special place. The water flowed by silently, swirling as it passed the fallen tree trunk. The dog ran on to the log and pawed at Colyn's carved name.

"This way, boy," Colyn said, setting off downstream.

He made his way along the edge of the river, cutting the bracken from his path with his knife. The dog followed behind, panting.

They found the dragon at the bend in the river, its body tangled in the branches of the fallen tree. All the leaves and twigs of the tree had burnt away and the branches were charred.

The dragon looked like a long, thick cable coiled and looped among the branches. It was burnt black all over.

Part of its belly sagged into the water and its tail trailed in the river, waving gently with the current. Some of its triangular-shaped scales hung loosely from its body and others had rubbed off and stuck to the branches of the tree. Its wings were completely gone. Its eyes had burnt away, too, and smoke wafted from the empty sockets. The whole carcass smouldered.

Colyn stared at the beast in amazement. It looked nothing like the picture of the dragon on his jigsaw puzzle. It did not have ridges on its tail or horns on its head. Nor was its mouth full of big, tearing teeth like a lion's. It had only four teeth—two jutting like tusks from its lower jaw and two dropping like fangs from its upper jaw. Its nostrils were flared like a pair of trumpets. Its neck was long and not much thicker than a man's thigh. It looked like a giant snake. Even its body was not very thick. If he had dared, Colyn could have touched his hands around its belly. It did not have four legs, either. It had only one pair where its tail joined its body, and they were short and muscular. Each foot had five large claws. The wings—or the burnt stumps where the wings had been—budded from its shoulders, but there were no front legs. It was nothing like the dragons Colyn had imagined. And yet ...

Colyn remembered the yellow eye he had seen through the mists of the window-stone, and the eye of the dragon on his puzzle. He looked at the dragon's raw eye-sockets and shuddered.

Suddenly the dog stopped nosing about and stared at the dragon. He grew rigid and began to growl.

"What's the matter, boy?" Colyn said. "You don't

41

nave to worry about him." He picked up a stone and threw it. "See?" he said, as the stone smacked into the dragon's neck.

It was then that Colyn saw. The dragon was not dead. Its head jerked up and swung towards him.

Colyn cried out and stumbled backwards. The dog barked. The dragon turned towards the sound, staring at the dog with its enormous empty eye-sockets. It opened its mouth as if to roar but only a gurgling sound came out.

Colyn looked about frantically. He found a long stick and began to sharpen it. The shavings seemed in a hurry to peel from the stick, and the point was sharp after a few strokes of the knife.

He held the spear at the ready and crept closer to the dragon. The beast tried to turn its head to follow the boy's movements but a branch got in the way. It banged at the branch wildly but lacked the strength to break it.

Creeping as close as he dared, Colyn took careful aim. He hurled the spear with all his might. It struck the dragon's right eye-socket and pierced its brain. The dragon writhed powerfully, snapping several branches, and lashed the river with its tail. A great wave of water hit Colyn, knocking him off his feet. Then the dragon shuddered and was still.

Without taking his eyes off the dragon, Colyn sat down, trembling. His dog whimpered and lay down beside him.

"Come on, boy," he said when he felt calmer. "We'd better get home."

His father was waiting when he entered the house.

"Where've you been?" he demanded. He was angry.

"I … er … I've just been down by the river," Colyn stammered.

His father looked at him strangely. "What doing?" he asked.

Colyn blushed. "Just looking," he said.

"You haven't done anything silly with that knife, have you?" His father nodded at the weapon in Colyn's belt.

"No," said Colyn. "I—"

"And you're wet!" his father interrupted.

"I … I slipped," Colyn said, knowing that he was telling a lie by telling only part of the truth.

"I ought to give you a hiding, son," his father said. "You know you're not to go down by the river without telling me. What if you'd drowned?" He was shouting, and Colyn was too young to understand that it was because he was frightened, frightened for the safety of his son.

"Besides," his father went on less loudly, "you're not to leave the house in the morning without having breakfast." He sat down on one of the kitchen chairs. He seemed to be tired suddenly. "What were you doing, anyway?" he asked.

Colyn was silent for a moment. He stared at his feet. "I was walking," he said. "With my dog."

His father sighed and looked at the dog. "Haven't you thought of a name for him yet?" he asked, trying to smile.

Colyn shook his head. "Not yet," he said. "I can't think of it."

"What about Rover?" his father suggested.

Colyn screwed up his nose. "That's a stupid name," he said.

His father looked hurt. "Well, you can't keep on calling him 'boy' for the rest of his life," he said.

Hearing his temporary name, the dog wagged his tail happily.

"Anyway," his father added, "hurry up and get changed and eat your breakfast. We're going to town today."

"Can we ride on the back of the truck?" Colyn asked, looking into his father's eyes.

"We?" his father teased.

"Oh, you know!" said Colyn. "Me and my dog!"

The boy and his dog rode on top of the potato sacks on the back of the truck. The dog sat on his haunches with his tongue out, looking into the wind. Colyn sat beside him, looking the other way.

The truck jolted along the gravel road. Soon they had passed the boundary of their own property. Trees whizzed past. Dandelions smeared yellow along the side of the road. Sheep looked up and ran away into the green and yellow paddocks. A horse cantered beside them until it had to stop at a fence.

Colyn hugged his dog. He felt deeply happy.

IX THE ENTRY

WHEN Colyn returned from town, he remembered the doorway he had made into the otherworld. He worked with his father for several hours in the afternoon, wondering all the while what he could do to stop the dragons coming out that night.

He decided that the best thing to do was to burn the cardboard box.

After he had finished his work, Colyn ran straight to the shed, his dog in tow. He walked around the box, considering the best way to hold it to drag it outside the shed. He put his fingers through the doorway to get a grip. But as he touched the cardboard he thought of the dragons. What if they were there, waiting to snap his fingers off? He pulled them out quickly.

He walked to the other side of the box and reached out to grab it with both arms. He latched his fingers around the corners and pulled. The box did not move. He pulled again, hard. His fingers slipped and he fell back on to his bottom, but the box did not budge. He bent his shoulder against it and pushed. It did not shift in the slightest.

He became frightened. He walked backwards and then ran at the box, bashing into it. It did not even wobble.

It was no use. He could not move it. He sat down to think. His dog trotted over to him and licked his face.

"Now what will we do, boy?" Colyn said.

He stroked his dog slowly, trying to think. "Well, at least we could make some more ammo," he said. And he got up and made six stones, which he put in his pockets, and six discs, which he stowed in his shirt. Then he sat down again and stared through the doorway.

He was still sitting, staring, when his father came into the shed.

"What's up?" he said. "Can't you think of anything to do?"

His father put one hand through the triangular doorway of the box and lifted it to one side. He set it down against the wall and nudged it flush with his foot.

Colyn gaped at him.

"You'll have to leave your cubby back here," his father told him. "Out of the way."

Colyn stood up and walked over to the box. He tried to lift it but failed.

"Dad," he said, "could you carry the box over to the rubbish heap for me? I want to burn it."

"Oh, you don't need to burn it," his father said. "It's out of the way here, that's the main thing."

"But I've finished playing with it," Colyn said. "I don't want it any more."

"You might want it tomorrow."

"No," said Colyn. He sounded almost rude and his father glanced at him sharply. "No, I don't want it any more. I want to burn it."

"You might change your mind," his father said. "Besides, it's still in pretty good nick. I might be able to use it for something some time, even with that hole in it."

"But Dad——!"

"Look, Colyn," his father interrupted. "You're not burning it and that's that!" He walked to the other side of the shed. "Now," he said. "Where's another shovel? I broke the handle of mine."

As Colyn's father stepped out of the shed with his new shovel, a terrible thing happened. The dog, who had been snuffling around at the back of the shed, discovered a rat. The rat scurried across the floor with the dog bounding after it. Seeing Colyn, the rat darted to one side and leaped through the doorway in the box.

Colyn cried out. But it was too late. The dog yapped once and jumped after the rat.

Without thinking, Colyn snatched his knife from his belt and stepped through the doorway too.

The white mists surrounded him. He could not see anything except his knife. Its black blade glowed like polished stone. He turned back to see the doorway. It was not there. He took several steps, groping like a blind boy, then stood still and listened.

Far off he could hear the dog barking. Stepping cautiously in the direction of the sound, he knocked something with his foot. He bent down to touch it and it slid away from him.

He stepped forward again, and in his frustration at not being able to see he slashed his knife in a line in front of his chest. The blade sliced the mist in two.

He gawked at the cut, expecting the mist to close over it. But it did not heal. There before him, at shoulder height, was a cut in the mist about a metre long. It was like a thin strip of clear glass on a frosted glass window.

Colyn put his eye to it. Through the gap he saw another world. He did not stop to consider how this could be. He walked forward, as if to step into it, but as he did so the white mist surrounded him again.

He waved his knife in frustration. There it was again: a slit in the mist. He looked through it, and it was like looking through a gap in frosted louvres. He saw his dog running across rocky ground towards a line of low hills. The dog had something in his mouth.

Colyn called. The dog paused for a moment and looked over his shoulder. He barked, ran a few paces back, then turned again and raced towards the hills. Colyn whistled but the animal did not stop.

Colyn stepped forward and the mist surrounded him once more. Tears of grief and rage sprang to his eyes.

"Oh, help me!" he cried. "Help me to get through!"

He swung his knife down at an angle, then across level with the ground, and then up at an angle until he had cut a triangle in the mist. It floated there in the whiteness, like a steel triangle hung from a stand in a percussion band, only larger and with all three corners joined.

Far away, a dragon roared. A dog barked. The mist within the triangle dissolved.

Colyn looked through the three-sided hole in the wall of mist. He took a deep breath and climbed through. Instantly he was in the otherworld. Wherever he looked it stretched on and on, as far as he could see.

There was no mist. There was no doorway. There was no way back.

X THE ESCAPE

COLYN stood on the shore of a great ocean. The shoreline was littered with small round pebbles. The water was light purple—mauve, like the colour of jacaranda flowers. Here and there it seemed to boil, as if great shoals of fish were churning it, but otherwise it was perfectly smooth.

Turning his back on the ocean, Colyn saw to the east a narrow rocky plain leading up to a line of low barren hills. Both the plain and the hills extended north and south, following the coast as far as the eye could see.

Through the slit in the mist Colyn had seen the dog running towards the hills. But he could not tell which hill he had headed for. He sighed, thrust his knife into his belt and set off.

The stones on the plain were small but sharp. Colyn could feel them through the soles of his boots. The ground shimmered in the heat. He began to sweat.

He trudged on without seeing a single living thing, not even a blade of grass. The hills were further away than he had thought. After walking for half an hour, he had covered barely half the distance.

When he reached the base of the hills he was quite thirsty. He found himself thinking that he should have tasted the mauve ocean water. Perhaps the seas were fresh in this world. He wondered if he should walk back.

As he was pondering this he noticed a black object lying on a nearby rock. He squinted at it. His heart began to beat faster. He walked over to it and, sure enough, it was a dead rat.

He cupped his hands to his mouth and called, "Here, boy! Here, boy!" His voice was swallowed up by the hills without so much as an echo.

He called again. Nothing. He put his fingers in his mouth and whistled, a loud, high whistle, as his father had taught him. There was no response.

He saw what appeared to be a rough path leading between two hills. It lay in shadow, and that in itself was enough to make Colyn decide to follow it.

He felt better once he was out of the heat of the sun. The path was easy to follow. It ran along the bottom of a wide, shallow valley. As he walked on, the hills became higher, and he realised that the valley path was leading him slowly but surely downward.

After walking for an hour, he sat down on a rock to rest. A lizard crept out of a crack near his foot. He kept quite still. The lizard crawled closer, stopping now and again to look up at him cautiously. It reminded him of the little brown skinks that lived on his veranda, except that there was an unusual lump on its back, right above its front legs. It looked as if it were wearing a knapsack. Colyn waited until it was within reach, then grabbed at it. The lizard hissed and leaped into the air, and as it did o the lump on its back opened out into two pairs of yellow wings. Colyn was startled, then astonished. He stared at the creature. It hovered briefly in front of him like a dragonfly, then zoomed away.

After the lizard had flown out of sight, Colyn noticed a faint roaring sound. He stood up and continued his journey along the valley.

The sound grew slowly louder. The valley changed direction sharply, swinging to the north. Colyn followed the path around the bend. It ran straight into a waterfall.

A sheet of white water blocked his path, spanning the entire width of the valley. But there was something strange about it. It poured over the top of the valley and tumbled down with great fury, but instead of falling into a pool or a river, the water fell straight into the ground. It hit the valley floor and disappeared without a splash. It looked like a white curtain, trimmed to touch the ground.

Colyn reached out. The water caught at his hand, knocking it down with great force. It splashed over his shirt, cooling him pleasantly. He cupped some in his hands and drank. It tasted good.

After he had satisfied his thirst, he looked around carefully. The waterfall was a dead end, and the valley walls were too steep to climb. He would have to go back. He felt like crying.

"Here, boy!" he called in desperation. Suddenly he felt frustrated that he did not have a proper name to call out. "Here, boy!" he yelled. But his voice was swallowed up by the noise of the rushing water. He called again but scarcely heard himself.

He took another drink and then began to travel back along the valley. He walked around the sharp bend and on towards the place where he had seen the flying lizard. The sound of the waterfall grew fainter.

Then he heard a sharp sound. A bark. He spun around to see his dog running towards him.

"Here, boy!" he called, squatting down to wait.

The dog bounded up and leaped on to him, knocking him over. He was wet, but Colyn was too happy to mind. He laughed and turned his head to stop the dog from licking his face.

It was then that a shadow passed over them. Instantly the dog and the boy forgot their play and looked up. A dragon was flying towards them. Because the sun was low, its shadow had gone before it as a warning.

Colyn scrambled to his feet and reached into his shirt for a disc. He threw it recklessly and it sped wide of its mark. The dragon did not even have to swerve to avoid it.

Two more dragons appeared over the horizon of the hills. The dog snapped and snarled ferociously, foam dripping from his mouth. He pranced up and down like a puppet jerking on a string.

The first dragon passed over again. As it did so it roared and snorted out two streams of flame from its flared nostrils. Colyn ducked, but the dragon was too high for its fire to scorch him.

The dragon began a third pass, and as it did so it swung into a dive. Colyn took careful aim and threw a round stone at its head. This time he was right on target. The beast swerved upwards abruptly and the _tone whizzed past beneath it.

Colyn hurled another stone and then another. As the dragon ducked the first, the second one struck it on the tail. The stone seemed to explode, like a hand grenade. It blew the tip of the dragon's tail right off.

The dragon bellowed in agony and flapped in a half circle before fleeing down the valley, towards the sea. It wobbled in flight like a giant butterfly. Colyn took aim and was about to throw another stone at it when his dog barked a warning.

He spun round to see a second dragon speeding towards him. It was gliding low along the valley, almost at head height, its mouth open, revealing its enormous fangs.

Colyn was off balance, so it was impossible for him to throw a stone. He staggered back, holding up his knife. But before the dragon could bite him his dog leaped into the air and latched on to its wing. He sank his teeth into the main wing-bone and held on. The dragon roared and began to roll in the air, trying to shake the dog off. In its pain and confusion, it spun out of control.

Suddenly the dog let go. He fell, hit the ground with a thump, and bounced along like an odd-shaped football.

The dragon hurtled into the hillside at the valley's bend. The ground shook with the force of the crash and stones tumbled down, forming an avalanche.

Colyn and his dog began to run. They raced past the dead dragon and around the bend. The waterfall loomed before them. Without hesitating, the dog jumped through the falling torrent.

Colyn sprang after him, plunging through the white water and into the white vapours. The mists blinded him, but he kept on running.

"Boy!" he shouted.

The third dragon swooped through the waterfall. Colyn heard the sound of the water as it struck the beast's wings—like the sound of a fire-hose squirting a giant umbrella—and then there was an eerie silence. He turned to see the dragon's great eyes shining like beacons in the fog. Ripping open his shirt he snatched a stone disc and hurled it at the dragon. As it left his hand it began to glow. It looked like a dragon's eye, speeding away from him. It smashed into the dragon's forehead. The beast bellowed, its eyes went out and it crashed to the invisible ground.

"Here, boy!" Colyn called urgently.

The dog nudged into him. Colyn reached down, caught his tail, and hung on. "All right, boy," he said. "Go!"

The dog ran and Colyn ran with him. Within minutes they were home, lying exhausted and dripping on the shed floor.

Colyn lay motionless for some time, catching his breath. His dog lay beside him, panting and licking himself. Colyn rolled his head to look at him.

"Dragon Biter," he said. "You saved my life."

COLYN was almost too tired to eat his tea. He sat at the table, knife and fork in hand, staring at his food.

His father broke the silence. "Where's your dog?" he asked.

Colyn poked at his mashed potato. "Dragon Biter?" he said wearily.

"What?" said his father, frowning.

Colyn looked up quickly. His face flushed. "Dragon Biter. I think that's his name," he said.

His father looked puzzled. "What made you think of a name like that?"

Colyn shrugged. "I don't know," he said.

"Dragon Biter," his father said slowly. "It sounds grand. But it's a bit long, don't you think? You need something short and snappy. Something you can call out. Perhaps you should just call him Dragon, or Biter."

Colyn did not say anything.

"Anyway," his father said, "where is he? He hasn't run off, has he?"

"He's in the shed."

"Must be about the first time I've seen you two apart," his father said. "Have you tied him up or something?"

"No. He's just staying in the shed tonight. I'll take him the bones after tea." He cut a piece of meat. "Did you know he caught a rat today?" he said.

"Did he?" His father was holding his fork half-way to his mouth. A piece of boiled carrot fell off the fork and bounced on the plate. He took no notice. "And didn't you say he caught one the other day?"

"Yes," said Colyn.

His father laughed. "Two in a week!" he said. "What a champion! We'll have to call him Rodent Snapper."

"No," said Colyn quietly. "His name is Dragon Biter."

After tea Colyn cleared the table, scraped the scraps into a dish and carried them down to the shed.

His dog was lying in front of the doorway to the otherworld, head on paws, looking forlorn. Colyn called his name softly: "Dragon Biter!"

The moment he said it, Colyn knew that his father was right. The name was too long. "It's the right meaning," he said to himself, "but not the right name."

The dog stood up and wagged his tail. Colyn scratched his neck roughly. "How are you, old boy?" he said. "Seen any dragons yet?"

The dog seemed to grin. He whacked Colyn's leg with his tail and woofed.

Colyn put the plate down and the dog began to eat hungrily. He gobbled up the scraps, then sniffed the boy's hand for more.

"No more, greedy guts," Colyn said, pushing him away.

The dog dabbed his knee with his damp nose.

"Aw, yuck!" Colyn said, laughing. He bent to wipe his leg and the dog licked his face. "Hey!" he cried, his heart as chirpy as a cricket.

Back in the house, he washed and dried the dishes quickly. After putting them away, he collected several potatoes and sliced and peeled them to make six flat stones and ten round stones.

"Now I'll be ready," he said.

He stole past his father and hid the stones under his bed. He changed, cleaned his teeth and went to the toilet, then kissed his father goodnight.

"What? Going to bed without being told?" his father laughed.

"I'm tired," Colyn said.

"You must be," his father said gently. "Have a good sleep, son. I'll see you in the morning."

Colyn tucked his knife under the pillow, laid his head on top of it, and fell asleep.

He was so exhausted that not even dreams could wake him, and yet he twisted and turned with dreams all night. His brain was brushed with bright colours and swift shapes. He saw the little lizard hovering on its yellow wings. He saw the great dragons diving at him. He saw his dog latched on to a dragon's wing. He saw the white wall of the waterfall. He saw a man standing, watching, beside a horse at the top of the falls. The man called something as the dog leaped through the torrent of water. It was a name, and Colyn heard it. It was the only sound he heard in the whole dream.

But the dream went on. A dragon followed him

through the waterfall, through the mists, and into his father's shed. It chased him to his special place by the river, and there it read his name.

When Colyn woke, the sky was light and his thoughts were clear. He remembered his own name in the wood, and he remembered the new name he had heard in his dream. He dressed quickly and quietly, putting his knife in his belt, and strode to the shed.

The dog was lying before the doorway, just as Colyn had left him. He was staring into the triangle, entranced. His ears twitched when Colyn stepped into the shed, but otherwise he lay quite still.

Colyn knelt to pat him. "So," he said, "we made it through the night. Did you get any sleep?" He thumped the dog's ribs. "Did you see any dragons, eh, Kinzar?"

At the sound of his name, the dog barked and wagged his tail furiously.

Colyn laughed and stood up. "Kinzar!" he said. The name rang against the iron roof. It sounded so right that Colyn wondered why he had not dreamed it before.

"I have to do something," he said when the dog had quietened down. "You coming?"

He set off towards the river. Once there, he made his way along the bank to his special place. He stood on the fallen log and looked at his name—COLYN LARKIN— carved in capitals in the weathered wood.

"I have to get rid of it," he said to Kinzar. "I don't know why, but it's dangerous. A dragon might see it and know who I am."

Taking his knife from his belt, Colyn set to work to scrape away the letters of his name. Wood shavings fell to the water and floated away like little boats. Before long there was only a flat place where his name had been.

Colyn stood up. "Well," he said, "it's done. My name's hidden but yours is found. A swap. Now let's get back before Dad gets up."

I**T was Sunday, a day for forgetting potatoes and lazing about. Colyn made toast and coffee for his father and took it to him on a tin tray. He was lying in bed with his hands behind his head, staring at the ceiling.

"Morning, boy," he said as Colyn entered the room.

"Hello, Dad," Colyn said. He waited for his father to sit up before he set the tray on the bed.

His father sipped the coffee. "Do you remember getting into bed with your mother and me on Sunday mornings?"

Colyn shook his head.

"No, I suppose not," his father said. "We used to cuddle you between us like a little, living teddy. Of course, you liked your mother best. There's nothing softer than a woman in a nightie, and children just have to snuggle in." He took another sip of his coffee and gulped as he swallowed. "Beds are full of dreams and memories," he said. "May all yours be sweet, son."

Colyn wanted to hug his father but he did not know how to do it without spilling the coffee, so instead he

61

said, "What are we going to do today, Dad?"

His father smiled. "What do you want to do?"

"Well," Colyn said, "do you remember that puzzle you told me about? The one that had the funny-looking dragons in it?"

"The one your mother and I did?"

"Yes. I want to do that."

His father thought for a moment. "I'm not sure I know where it is," he said. "I haven't done any jigsaw puzzles since your mother died. Not till the other day, anyway."

"But you could look for it," Colyn urged. "I could help you find it."

"I'll tell you what," his father said. "You go and tidy up the lounge-room table, then take your dog for a run. That'll give me time to get up and have a shower and look for the puzzle."

"I've thought of a name for him," Colyn said. "I'm going to call him Kinzar."

"What? I thought you were going to call him Dragon Biter."

"It's too long. Kinzar is better."

"Kin-zar," his father said slowly. "Yes. It sounds nice. Sort of smooth. Where did you get a name like that?"

"In my dreams," Colyn said.

"Oh," said his father. He did not know what else to say, so he said, "Well, then, you take Kinzar for a trot while I get up and get organised."

Colyn was excited. He tidied the table quickly and then ran outside, with Kinzar yapping beside him. He ran very fast, but he could not tell whether his heart was racing because of the excitement or the exercise.

"Come on, slowcoach!" he said to Kinzar. And he ran faster, down the gravel road alongside the potato paddock, up to their boundary fence and back, the dog skipping and snapping at his heels.

He was puffing and Kinzar was panting when they entered the house. His father smiled and held up a bulging brown-paper bag.

"Found it!" he said happily. "At least, I think this is the one." He poured the puzzle pieces on to the big jarrah table. "I can't remember what happened to the box," he said. "In fact, I can't remember ever seeing one. Never mind. It makes it all the more challenging to do a puzzle without a picture to copy from."

Colyn and his father set to work finding the straight-edged pieces.

"Keep your eyes peeled for pieces with the same colours, too," his father said.

It took them over an hour to sort through the pieces and find the ones with straight edges. By the time they had finished, they also had several piles of pieces that seemed to go together. One heap had pieces with blue on them for the sky. Another had pieces with brown on them for the earth and rocks. Another had bits of people and horses. And the final pile had bits of dragons—bits of scaly bodies and leathery wings and glary eyes and fiery nostrils.

"Now for a cup of tea before we begin," his father said. "Want one?"

Colyn nodded. "Yes please."

When his father returned with the mugs of tea and a

plate of biscuits, Colyn had already fitted together a dozen pieces of the bottom edge of the puzzle. There was a hoof in one of the pieces, and an arrow-head in another.

"Off to a good start," his father said. "Now, let's see." And he began to work on the sky.

By lunchtime the border was completed. It was going to be a big picture. It was almost as long and as wide as the table.

"Let's have a break for lunch," his father suggested.

"No," Colyn said. "I'm not hungry."

"Have a break anyway, son. You'll come back to it fresher."

Sitting at the kitchen table, Colyn gulped his food.

"Slow down! You're eating like a dog!" his father said. "Anyone would think there was a pack of mongrels looking over your shoulder waiting to pounce on your food."

But Colyn could not slow down, so his father let him be.

When he had finished, he pushed his plate into the middle of the table, scraped his chair back, and turned to leave.

"Hey, hang on!" his father said. "That's not where you leave your plate."

Colyn put his plate in the sink and looked at his father pleadingly.

His father shook his head and laughed. "Go on, then," he said.

With the border done, it was difficult to work out what to do next. Colyn began to look through the dragon pieces.

"It's a bit early for those," his father said as he came up to the table with his cup of tea. "We'll need to keep working in from the edges. You work on the ground and I'll work on the sky."

Colyn looked at the dragon pieces longingly. "The dragons will be in the air," he said. "Can't I do the sky?"

"All right. No worries."

It was hard going. The puzzle had thousands of pieces, and Colyn and his father had no picture to guide them. So many pieces were brown with the earth or blue with the sky that it was difficult to tell them apart.

After an hour Colyn had finished a second row of pieces along the top of the puzzle. Scraps of wings floated like ash in the blue sky. His father had managed to work a little faster on the ground. The brown earth was spiked with the legs of horses and strewn with broken weapons.

By late afternoon Colyn had pieced together an entire dragon wing in the top right corner of the puzzle. He no longer looked for pieces of the sky. He sorted through the pile of dragon parts, searching for the pieces that would make up this dragon. He could tell from the size of the wing that it was a big one, and he wanted to see it.

His father was now concentrating on the bottom right corner, where he had completed the hind legs and haunches of a white stallion.

"I think your horse is rearing up at my dragon," Colyn said.

"Yes," his father said. "I wonder who's riding it?" He snapped another piece in place. "It's funny," he said, "but I don't remember any of this. I remember doing the puzzle with your mother. And I remember it pictured dragons and horsemen. But I don't remember a single specific detail."

Neither Colyn nor his father was hungry when teatime came, so they worked on. It began to grow dark but neither of them thought to turn the light on. They squinted at the pieces and bent their faces closer to the table. Only when it was almost too dark to see did Colyn reach up and flick on the light switch.

"There!" he said.

The dragon was done. Its wings filled the entire top right corner of the puzzle. Its tail vanished off the edge of the picture, but its great serpentine neck bent down towards the rider, and flames spouted from its nostrils. Colyn's father had not yet finished the rider—his head and shoulders were missing—so it was impossible to tell how or if he survived the attack.

Father and son looked at the dragon in silence. It was an ugly and awesome sight. Its enormous wings were black and leathery, and ribbed like a bat's. Its legs and talons dangled from its body awkwardly and dangerously. Its neck was long and snakelike, and covered, like its body, with triangular scales. Its nostrils flared like trumpets and tusks jutted from its lower jaw. Its mouth gaped to reveal a forked tongue and two fangs. Its great eyes were canary yellow, with black, perpendicular slits for pupils. Evil seemed to shine from them—not only at the headless rider, but at Colyn and his father, too.

Colyn's father rubbed his eyes and sighed. "It's late," he said. "You'd better have some tucker and hit the sack."

"But Dad!" Colyn protested. "I want to see the rider. I want to see what he looks like and how he is going to kill the dragon."

His father shook his head. "It's too late, son. I might do a bit more while you're asleep. You can see the rider in the morning." He bent to look at the dragon again. "I told you they were funny looking, didn't I?" he said. "Have you ever seen anything like that before?"

"Yes," Colyn said, very quietly.

XIII THE VISITOR

IN his sleep, Colyn dreamed that there was a hand on his shoulder. He turned over, holding the blankets tightly. There it was again—on the other shoulder: a hand, shaking him gently but urgently.

He opened his eyes. His bedroom was in blackness, but it was the blackness of early morning when the night is thinned with the first promises of light. He blinked and rubbed his eyes. The shapes in the room came into faint focus. The hand let go of his shoulder.

Colyn felt a sudden rush of fear. A man who was not his father was standing by his bed. There was not enough light to see his features properly but he was tall and had a beard. His eyes and teeth showed whitely in the darkness.

In panic, Colyn sat upright and grabbed under his pillow for his knife. He thrust it at the stranger.

The man stepped back and bowed. "Rykone," he said. "I am Wayth of the Kinroan. We guarded the doorway while you slept."

Colyn was confused. "What? Who are you?"

"I am Wayth of the Kinroan," the man repeated. His

accent was strange but understandable, and his voice was deep and sure. "I am sorry to wake you, Rykone. We know of your battle in the Falls Valley. We suspect your weariness. But it is the dawning and you must come now."

Colyn kept his knife at the ready and eyed the stranger warily. "You are from the otherworld?"

The man nodded.

"But how did you find me?"

"We knew a doorway had been opened between the worlds," Wayth said. "We sent out scouts. They saw kinoi, dragons, flying in the bright light of mid-morning." Wayth shook his head. "Dragons in the daylight. That is always a sign of great danger.

"One of our scouts ventured near the Falls Valley. He saw three dragons circle in battle formation, then swoop into the valley. While he was riding to the place of battle he saw one dragon rise above the hills, wounded. He felt another crash into a side of the valley. He rode swiftly and arrived above the falls in time to see a dog and a boy and a dragon disappear through the falling waters." Wayth spread his arms and concluded simply, "This is how we learned the way, Rykone."

"But the mists," said Colyn. "How could you see?"

"Our ears were our eyes," Wayth said. "Kinzar has a clear voice." He stooped to pat Kinzar, and the dog wagged his tail.

Colyn suddenly realised that Kinzar had been standing quietly beside the stranger from the beginning. He glanced from the dog to the man, then lowered his knife.

"Kinzar," he called, patting the bed.

The dog looked at Wayth, as if asking permission, then leaped on to the bed. Colyn put his arm around his neck.

"Kinzar trusts you," Colyn said.

"Yes." The man chuckled. "He knows me."

There were so many things Colyn wanted to ask. His head spun with questions. "What does his name mean?" he asked, nestling his face in Kinzar's fur.

"Kinos Izar—Dragon Biter."

"Oh," Colyn exclaimed. "And who are the Kinroam?"

"The Kinroan," Wayth corrected him. "We are the people who live in the Middle Plains. Our name means Dragon Slayers." He looked at the window. "It's getting light," he said. "We must get back while the dragons sleep. There is much to be done."

Colyn got out of bed and began to dress. He pulled his pyjama-top over his head without unbuttoning it and fumbled for his shirt. It was cold and he shivered as he did up the buttons.

"Were you on guard all night?" Colyn asked.

"Yes," said Wayth. "Since dusk. We killed one dragon. Four dragons we wounded, one mortally, we think. The others retreated to their lairs. None entered Nalkrist."

"Nalkrist?" said Colyn.

"Your world," Wayth said. "We kept them out."

"A dragon came three nights ago," Colyn said. "It flew over our house. Kinzar woke me and I killed it."

"With your knife?"

"No. With a stone I made with my knife."

"So," said Wayth, stroking his beard absently. "You

have killed *two* dragons."

"*Three*, I think," Colyn said. "The one that fell into the river. The one in the valley ... Oh, but Kinzar killed that one ... And the one that chased me through the waterfall. I threw a flat stone at it. I *think* I killed it, because its eyes stopped shining."

Wayth shook his head. "I have been a warrior for fourteen years and I personally have killed only eight dragons."

Without seeming to move, Wayth stood suddenly straighter, as if every muscle in his body had tensed for action.

"These stones," he said. "Do you have more?"

"Yes, I made some last night," Colyn said. "And I can make more easily."

"Then if you please, do it quickly, Rykone."

Colyn noted how Wayth bowed his head slightly when he said this name. He reached under his bed to get the round and flat stones.

"What does Rykone mean?" he asked, tucking his shirt into his pants and thrusting the round stones into his pockets.

"It means Knife Lord," Wayth said. "It is an ancient title for the one who holds the Kinrye, the Dragon Knife." He motioned towards the door. "Please, Rykone," he said. "We have no time."

Colyn took a step forward, then stopped. "But where are we going?" he asked.

"To Klarin. To my world," said Wayth.

"But why?"

"You must close the doorway."

Colyn felt suddenly distressed. "But I can't!" There was a note of panic in his voice. "I can't! I don't know where the *door* is!"

Wayth patted Colyn's shoulder. "Do not be alarmed, Rykone. We found the door three days ago."

Colyn gasped. Yet in spite of his surprise his thoughts were calm and clear. "Then why can't *you* close it?" he asked.

"It should be closed by the one who opened it," Wayth answered.

"But how did you know *I* made it?"

Wayth laughed. "It can only be done with the Dragon Knife," he said. "And you have the knife."

"Oh," Colyn exclaimed.

"Please, Rykone. Come."

Colyn gave in. He stepped in front of Wayth and led the way to the kitchen. The house was lit up with a grey half-light. As they passed through the lounge-room, Wayth paused to look at the unfinished puzzle on the table.

Colyn raised the kitchen blind to let in more light from the whitewashed sky. He glanced at Wayth and noticed for the first time that he was armed. He wore a sword in a scabbard on his back and a dagger in a sheath at his side. He was tall and muscular, his leather breast-plate emphasising the power of his chest and arms. A woven headband kept his long hair from his eyes. His face, so far as Colyn could make it out in the faint light, seemed both stern and kind.

Colyn collected some small potatoes and began to peel them. Wayth watched, fascinated, as the skin fell away and the newly-white tubers turned to stone in Colyn's hands.

"I will carry some," Wayth said, taking one and weighing it in his hand. "It would be wise to be well armed. If the doorway is not sealed by nightfall we will have to fight. And it will not be a few dragons this time."

Colyn sliced several large potatoes, peeled the slices, then slid them into his shirt. He crammed the round stones into his pants pockets until they bulged uncomfortably. He dumped the peelings in the scrap bucket, then cleaned the blade of his knife on a tea-towel and poked it through his belt.

Wayth took the stones that were left over and stowed them in his own pockets.

Before leaving the house, Colyn peeped into his father's bedroom. His father was fast asleep, his head half off the pillow, his mouth half open, his chin rough with stubble, and his hair ruffled.

As he looked at his father, Colyn felt a deep love stir in his heart. He wanted to go and hug him. Instead, he whispered simply, "Goodbye, Dad," and tiptoed away.

XIV THE SCOUTS

Wayth stepped through the doorway into the otherworld. Colyn followed him. Hardly had the mists covered them before Colyn heard voices.

"Wayth!" he called.

"Don't be afraid, Rykone," Wayth said. "These are my brothers, scouts and warriors of the Middle Plains."

"Rykone!" a dozen voices said in salutation.

Although he could not see them, Colyn imagined the men bowing slightly, as Wayth had done. They began to talk in a language he did not understand.

"Rykone," Wayth said, his voice seeming to come from the mist itself, "we don't know the way back. Two of our men set out but have not returned."

"I know a way," Colyn said. He drew his knife and, seeing the weapon but not the hand that held it, the Kinroan murmured in amazement.

Colyn cut a large triangle in the swirling whiteness. For a few seconds the three slits floated in the mist, revealing glimpses of the otherworld; then the mist within the triangle dissolved, opening a doorway. The

Kinroan exclaimed at the wonder of it.

Colyn placed one leg through the opening. He could see it dangling there as if it were an object by itself, unattached to a body. Before he could step through, he felt a hand on his shoulder.

"But the two who are lost?" Wayth said.

Colyn pulled his leg back. "I don't know how to help," he said.

Wayth said simply, "Try, Rykone."

"Perhaps ..." Colyn said. His voice trailed away as he thought. "Yes, it might work."

He reached into his shirt, withdrew a stone disc and flung it up. It sped away, growing brighter as it rose higher. He threw another, then a third.

The light of the three moons barely pierced the mists. Colyn could just make out the faces of several of the closest Kinroan. He felt a deep frustration.

"The mists are too thick," he said.

"Perhaps Kinzar could find them," Wayth suggested.

Colyn brightened up. "Yes!" he said excitedly. "Yes, of course he could. He can see in this stuff as good as a dragon!"

He called the dog. "Kinzar," he said, "two men are lost. Fetch them. Go on, boy! Find them!"

Kinzar trotted off soundlessly. Colyn glimpsed his tail, held upright in the moons' thin light like a tattered banner.

The company stood in silence for a few minutes, listening intently, but they heard no sound.

"We cannot wait," Wayth said. "We must get back. The day is too short already." Then he added, "With the moons and the dog to guide them they will return if they are alive."

The doorway Colyn had cut had disappeared, so he cut another and stepped through on to the pebbled beach. He turned to watch the Kinroan materialise into their own world.

Colyn's heart sank as the Kinroan came into view. The first man was unhurt but terribly tired. He slumped down on the beach, exhausted. The second man was badly burnt on his knife arm. The third man seemed unhurt himself but he carried across his shoulders another man, who was dead. And so it went on.

Lastly, Wayth stepped through. He looked at his warriors sitting or lying on the beach. There were seventeen in all. Five were wounded, three were dead.

The dead men had been laid side by side and now their comrades gathered around them. Wayth looked at each corpse in turn, then he selected six smooth stones from the shore and placed them on their blind eyes.

When Wayth had finished, Colyn began to cry. "I didn't know," he sobbed. "I didn't know you'd been hurt."

"Rykone," Wayth said gently, putting an arm around the boy, "this is war. We knew we would be hurt before we began. That is the price of the prize—the price of your freedom and ours. It is a price we are prepared to pay."

He hugged Colyn tightly, then stood back. "Remember this, Rykone. There are some things worth dying for and there are some things not worth living without."

"But it's all my fault!" Colyn sobbed. "If I hadn't cut

the door—"

"The dragons would still be here and we would still be fighting them, only for some other reason," Wayth interrupted. "And," he added, "if you hadn't cut the door you wouldn't know of our world. Now perhaps some day *you* will be able to help *us*."

Colyn rubbed his eyes. "What do you mean?" he asked.

Wayth shrugged. "Our legends speak of a Rykone. Perhaps they speak of you."

One of the Kinroan stepped over to Wayth and touched his shoulder. "Look," he said, pointing towards the distant hills.

Colyn turned with Wayth. Brown smoke was rising from the plain. Colyn peered intently. The smoke became dust. It was moving towards them.

"Riders," the man said. "I hope they have plenty of mounts."

"They know our numbers," Wayth said. "They will have enough."

"I wonder how they have fared with the door," the first man said.

Colyn's ears pricked up. "Have they got the door with them?" he asked.

Wayth laughed. "They wouldn't be riding at that speed if they were dragging the door."

Colyn looked puzzled. "Dragging it?"

"Yes!" Wayth said. "We harness four horses to the task. When one team tires, we hitch another. We began the journey two days ago, when our scouts reported your battle and your route of escape. It is a long way from the

Middle Plains to the falls, but they should have been able to continue through the night unhindered. The dragons were thinking of you last night, not the door. And besides, they don't know—or didn't know—that we have it."

As Wayth spoke, Kinzar leaped into the world. He stood on the beach, wagging his tail and panting. A hush fell on the Kinroan as they looked anxiously to see if the two lost men would follow him. But they did not. The warriors murmured their disappointment.

Wayth bent to pat Kinzar. "So," he said. "They are dead. Or as good as." He straightened up. "Five warriors lost out of nineteen," he said. "And the battle not yet begun."

In their sadness, Colyn and the Kinroan watched the brown cloud draw nearer. Horses and their riders appeared in the dust, at first flickeringly, then solidly. Kinzar ran out to meet them, barking across the shimmering plain. The figures grew larger and larger until they were life-sized and standing among the scouts on the beach.

XV THE RIDERS

THERE were ten riders and each one held the reins of two riderless mounts, making thirty horses in all.

Colyn was dazzled by the horses. He had never seen such beautiful, majestic animals. They were tremendously large yet exquisitely featured, and seemed to combine the strength and size of draught-horses with the speed and delicacy of racehorses. They were mostly brown—a rich chocolate brown—but some had patches of white on them and one was completely white. In spite of their long, dusty journey from the hills, their coats shone and they looked fresh.

The leader dismounted. He looked casually at Colyn, but the moment he spotted the knife in the boy's belt, he stood to attention and bowed.

"Rykone!" he said.

The title caught the attention of the other riders. They looked at Colyn, dismounted, and bowed too.

Colyn was not sure what to do. He nodded at them and then looked to Wayth for guidance.

The riders stood before Colyn as if waiting to be

dismissed. When he said nothing, they broke away in ones and twos and approached their friends.

It was then that Colyn realised that several of the riders were different from the rest. He stared at them. They were shorter, a little bigger around the hips, and their leather breastplates were shaped differently.

Noticing his stares, one of the riders came over to him.

"You are surprised to see women armed for war, Rykone?" she asked.

Colyn swallowed and nodded.

"These are hard times," the woman said. "Our men do not willingly recruit us for war. They are not without love or valour. But now they are too few to protect all the Kinroan hold precious. So we must fight beside them, or all will be lost."

As she spoke, Wayth came to her side and grinned. Colyn suddenly noticed that, like the woman, he had a blue ribbon tied to his arm, just below the shoulder.

"I see you have met the captain of the archers, Rykone," Wayth said.

The woman smiled. "I am Insay," she said. Then she did something Colyn's mother might have done were she alive. She reached out and brushed the hair from his forehead and caressed his cheek.

"So young," she said quietly. "I have a daughter about your age. I'm glad she's not here." She turned away abruptly and went to her horse.

Wayth watched her go, and kept watching.

Colyn touched his arm to catch his attention. "Why do you wear a ribbon?" he asked.

"It's a mark of rank," Wayth replied, turning to him.

"I am captain of the scouts."

The riders had food and medicine, and they gave out each as it was needed. Someone gave Colyn a chunk of black bread and a slice of strong-smelling cheese. But he could not eat. His throat seemed to have closed up so that he could not swallow, and he had to spit out the bread he had bitten off. Around him the Kinroan were eating like wolves.

Taking Colyn with him, Wayth stepped over to the leader. "It's good to see you, Naim," he said.

"I wish I could say the same for you," Naim said, looking at the weary and wounded men. "Three dead," he said, nodding at the corpses.

"And two lost in the mists," Wayth said.

Naim looked at all the men in turn. "The sons of Ekome," he said gravely.

"Yes," said Wayth. "The two brothers. Lost as they lived. Together."

"They were the last of Ekome's sons," Naim said. "Who will know her grief?"

There were tears in Wayth's eyes. "Yes," he said. "Who will know?" Then he blinked and said briskly, "Well, what news?"

"You tell me first," Naim said.

"You can see what we have to tell," Wayth said. "But it's not all one sided. We killed one dragon and wounded four. They didn't expect us at the doorway and so we kept them from Nalkrist and the Rykone and the Kinrye."

When he realised that Wayth had finished what he wanted to say, Naim said, "We saw the dragons come back just before dawn. Our scouts said they came as they

81

went, through the falls. The scouts waited for you there with horses. When you didn't return we began to think that you were lost. That the worlds were lost."

"Always looking on the bright side, Naim!" Wayth laughed. "No, we weren't lost. The skirmish was hard and it took me a while to wake and convince the Rykone."

Naim glanced at Colyn and said quietly, but not so quietly that Colyn could not hear, "He's so young! I expected ... I don't know. But not a boy!"

"He has the knife and with it the power," Wayth said. "If it is so now, think what he will become, with all his youth and manhood ahead of him."

Naim nodded. "I will tell you something strange, though," he said. "Our main company was entering the valley when the dragons rose above the hills from the falls. They must have seen us from that height, but they ignored us and flew on."

"So! You have reached the valley!" Wayth cried triumphantly.

"Oh, yes. Before dawn," Naim said. "They will be half way along it by now."

"By the Plains, we'll do it yet!" Wayth said. "Come on, let's get going."

He strode to the magnificent white stallion and took hold of the reins. "Mount up!" he called.

At the command the company sprang to life. Men and women dashed to and fro, finding and mounting their horses. Several Kinroan led horses to the three dead men. They slung the bodies over the saddles and lashed them tightly so that they would not fall.

Wayth surveyed the action from his saddle, his horse snorting and prancing, wanting to be off. Then he noticed Colyn standing amid the confusion. He spurred his horse forward, grasped the reins of a free horse and rode to Colyn.

"Can you ride, Rykone?"

"A bit," Colyn said.

"Mount up then, master!" he said. "This mare's made for unsure riders. She's gentle as a mother."

Colyn could not reach the stirrup. The horse was too tall. Wayth dismounted and helped the boy into the saddle. The stones grated in his pockets like big marbles as he swung his leg over the animal's broad back.

Once seated, he felt terribly small. He looked down to see Kinzar dodging between the horse's legs. The mare stepped sideways nervously, and Colyn rolled in the saddle like a leaf lifted by a wave. He clung to the horse's mane.

"Kinzar!" he scolded. "Stop it! Kinzar!"

The dog moved away, hanging his head and curling his tail between his legs.

Naim called out and the company set off across the stony plain to the hills. They rode at a canter, and as they did so they formed themselves into a column of ten deep and three abreast. Colyn rode in the first half of the column, between Wayth and Naim. Insay and the other two women rode in front of them.

Colyn was surprised at how smoothly the mare ran and how easily he was able to ride her. He imagined he was on a giant greyhound, lolloping along with great, smooth bounds.

The Kinroan had long hair which fluttered out as they rode. Once in the saddle each warrior seemed to become part of his or her horse, moving with it in perfect harmony.

After settling into an easy rhythm, the riders began to chat with each other. Snatches of conversation drifted back to Colyn.

"... And look at his size!" one woman said. "He's as scrawny as a skinned rabbit!"

Wayth heard the woman's comment. He winked at Colyn, then called out, "Kinroan! Remember of whom you speak!"

The woman who had spoken half twisted in her saddle to look back at Wayth and Colyn. "Your pardon, Rykone," she said. "I was only saying ..." Her voice trailed away and she rode on in silence.

Insay turned and grinned mischievously at Wayth. "Bully!" she said.

The hills drew effortlessly nearer. Colyn remembered his first and last journey across this barren plain on foot. It is much better on horseback, and with friends! he thought. He looked down at the ground to see the stones spin from his horse's hoofs. He felt happy—happy as the day he had found the knife—happy as the day he had made Kinzar.

"I've been thinking," Wayth said.

"Oh-ho!" said Naim.

Wayth continued seriously. "You said the dragons must have seen you entering the valley, and yet they ignored you."

"Yes," Naim nodded, growing serious himself.

"Well, that must mean they don't know we have the door," Wayth said.

"Perhaps," Naim replied. "Or it could simply mean they have something big in store for us. They now know to their cost that we know about the door*way*. They know our main force is headed for the falls. They have brains to add it up. I would be disappointed in them if they hadn't guessed by now."

"Why do the dragons want the door?" Colyn asked.

"To keep open the way between the worlds," Wayth said. "They want to be able to enter Nalkrist at will. They have spirit companions there."

"Spirit companions?" The term did not make sense to Colyn.

"You call them demons," Wayth said. "They are the same as dragons, only they have no bodies, so you have to fight them with different weapons. Your demons and our dragons—they would make a terrible alliance."

"Yes, they want to keep the doorway open," Naim agreed. "And they want the Kinrye."

"*My* knife!"

"Yes. The Dragon Knife."

"But why?" Colyn asked.

"They made it," Wayth said. "They forged it with the flame of their nostrils and the cunning of their hearts."

Colyn caught his breath.

"Don't be alarmed," Wayth said. "A knife is a power for good or evil according to the heart of the wielder, not the maker."

Naim nodded. "It's true. The Kinrye has great power over the dragons. And it's the only knife that can open a door between the worlds."

Colyn thought for a moment. "Dragons may have made it," he said, "but it's my knife now."

"Yes, Rykone," Wayth said. There was a mixture of warmth and sadness in his voice. "Yes, it's your knife now. And we must close the doorway you made with it so that you can keep it safe for both our worlds, safe for the day of need."

COLYN was tired, and the rhythmic movement of his horse had lulled him into a half sleep. He and the Kinroan had travelled well into the valley without incident. Insay had replaced Naim at his side but had hardly spoken to him. Kinzar trotted just in front of his horse, his tongue lolling from the side of his mouth like a scarf.

"When did Kinzar come to you?" Wayth asked.

Colyn was staring at the hoofs of the horse in front of him, watching them rise and fall without even realising that he was seeing them. He blinked and looked up. "What?" he said.

"Kinzar. When did he come to you?"

"Oh," said Colyn. "I made a carving about a week ago. Not yesterday, but the Sunday before."

"Did you carve other dogs?" Wayth asked.

"I tried," Colyn said.

"Three times?" Wayth asked.

Colyn looked at him in surprise. "Yes."

"And you burned two and threw the other in the water?"

"Yes!" Colyn said, straightening up in the saddle. "How did you know?"

"Three dogs died in our village the week before last," Wayth said. "One leaped into a cooking fire, one fell into a pit fire and one fell off a log into the river and never surfaced. It's a funny thing. Dogs die, of course. But I have never known a dog to die by fire or by water before."

"I did that?" Colyn asked, shocked at the thought.

"Perhaps," Wayth nodded. After riding a few paces, he added, "Then Kinzar went missing."

"I thought I made him with my knife," Colyn said. "He looks exactly the same as the dog I carved, only bigger."

"It's not in a human's power to create life," Wayth said. "Not even with *that* knife." He nodded at the weapon in Colyn's belt. "No, you didn't make him. But you did something almost as mysterious. You called him through the wood."

"But how could—?"

Colyn's question was interrupted by the whinnying of horses at the front of the column. Frightened by the horses' hoofs, a cloud of little lizards had burst into the air, flashing their bright yellow wings and hissing. Several horses shied, bringing the whole column to a halt, and it took the riders several moments to steady them.

"Those blasted oikina!" Wayth cursed. "I wish I could swat every last one of them!"

"But they're so beautiful!" Colyn protested.

"Beauty and goodness don't always go together," Insay

88

said. "We think the oikina, the dragonettes, spy on us for the dragons."

Colyn had almost forgotten that Insay rode beside him. He turned in his saddle to look at her. At a glance he knew that goodness and beauty met together in her. He blushed and felt suddenly awkward.

"I saw one—a dragonette, I mean—the first time I was here," he said. "I tried to catch it but it flew off. A little while later the dragons attacked."

"It could be coincidence," Insay said. "It's a long way from the Falls Valley to the Mountain Lairs. A dragonette would take almost a day to fly there."

"Yes, but it wouldn't take one long to find a patrol," Wayth said.

"Anyway, these can't do us any harm," said Insay. "They can't tell the dragons anything about us that they don't already know."

As soon as the lizards scattered and the horses settled, the company began to travel on.

Perhaps because he was feeling drowsy, Colyn said, "I had a dream about my name the other night. I dreamed that a dragon read it where I carved it on a log."

Wayth looked at the boy sharply. "Was it a true dream?"

His alarm made Colyn alert. "I don't know," he said. "It was the same night I dreamed Kinzar's name. And that was true."

"But have you carved your name somewhere?" Insay asked. "With that knife?"

"Yes. But after the dream I scratched it off."

Insay sighed with relief. "It was a presentiment, a

forewarning. You did well to heed it."

"But what does my name matter?" Colyn asked.

"It may be different in your world, but in Klarin there's power in a name," Wayth said. "Somehow it possesses the person it belongs to." He shrugged. "No one can quite explain it."

"But my name's not special," Colyn said. "Lots of people are called——"

Wayth interrupted him. "Don't speak it!" he said sternly. "Not even to me." Then he relaxed and added quietly, "You can't tell how a name has power, Rykone. It might be the way it's said, or the way it's spelt, or the way it's joined to another name, or the way it links you to the people who owned it before you."

"But you call me Rykone and I call you Wayth. Why is that all right?"

"Rykone is a title," Wayth said. "It goes with the knife. Everyone knows that, friend or foe. In speaking your title we say nothing an enemy cannot see with his own eyes. And as for Wayth, it is merely my common name."

Colyn began to muse on his name. "Oh!" he exclaimed at last. "Klarin!" He was hardly aware that his thoughts were slipping through his lips. "My last name's got the same letters, only swapped around."

Wayth, if he heard, did not respond.

Colyn was beginning to feel saddle-sore. The whole company was silent. Everyone seemed too weary or too disheartened to talk. Colyn wanted to know hundreds of things about the Kinroan and their world. But for the moment he could not think of a single thing to ask. His brain felt as numb as his bottom.

The brooding silence of the riders was broken by shouts from the valley walls. Colyn looked up to see several Kinroan, all women, standing high up on either side of the valley. They were waving and shouting greetings.

The climbers had strung a rope across the valley, and had hung a net from the rope. The net was fine, like a fishing net, so Colyn did not notice it until he was quite close. It hung down almost to the height of the riders and drifted in the slight breeze.

Wayth smiled at Colyn. "They're hanging a dragon net," he said. "It's a slow business, and a gamble, but it often pays off."

"But it looks too thin," Colyn said.

"It's a mist net," Insay said. "It doesn't have to be strong, just invisible. When a dragon hits it at speed, it comes away from the rope and tangles in the wings."

As they passed under the net, one of the riders reached up and tugged it. The women above yelled, and the riders yelled back. Both parties kept hurling insults at each other cheerfully until they were out of earshot.

The sight of the climbers had put life back into the riders. They were talking together again. And there was a sense of excitement as they realised that they must be quite close to the main war party.

The dullness had been banished from Colyn's thoughts, too. He began to remember the questions he wanted answered. He turned to Insay.

"How come you all know about my knife?" he asked.

"It was hidden in your world long ago for safe-

91

keeping," Insay said. "Many of our legends speak of it. But no one had seen it until seven years ago."

"Seven years ago? Did you see it then?"

Insay hesitated and glanced at Wayth. "Yes, we saw it then," she said. "A woman brought it from Nalkrist."

Colyn caught his breath and felt for the knife in his belt. "*My* knife?"

Insay nodded. "The Dragon Knife, the Kinrye."

"She brought it back to Klarin," Wayth said.

"The Rykona," Insay said lovingly. "The Knife Lady."

"She made a door by accident, like you," Wayth said. "But she didn't lose it, so Nalkrist was not endangered. She visited us often.

"At first she knew nothing of her power. But the knife fitted her palm. She learned quickly and helped us win several battles. But then the dragons came against us in full strength, determined to kill her and capture the knife. We fought for her, and she fought for us, but she died in the great battle."

Wayth paused, then said bitterly, "We killed many dragons that day, the day we lost the Rykona. And they killed many Kinroan. Too many."

"Most of our men died in that battle," Insay said. "We women call it the Turning War. For since that day we have turned to war to strengthen the men who remain."

"But how did my knife get back into my world if the Rykona died here?" Colyn asked.

"The two eldest sons of Ekome took her body back to Nalkrist, with the Kinrye," Insay said. "At least, that is what they set out to do. We didn't know if they'd succeeded until this week, when you made the door and brought the Kinrye back. For you see, they never returned. They must have lost their way in the mists, like their younger brothers today."

Colyn felt strangely, terribly torn. Tears were rolling down his cheeks. But he could not tell whether he was crying for the Kinroan who had died in the great battle, or Wayth and Insay who had loved and lost the Rykona, or the Rykona who had fought and died bravely, or the sons of Ekome who were lost in the mist, or Ekome whom he did not know and whose grief was soon to be unknowable, or himself who could not remember his mother. He was simply swallowed up in sadness and loss.

Insay looked at Colyn, and tears spilled from her eyes too. "There are many things I would like to tell you about the Rykona," she said. "But I would have to sit quietly with you and cradle you in my arms to do it." She reached over to embrace him but the movements of their horses were unevenly matched and turned her attempt to comfort him into clumsiness.

As Insay released Colyn, the company rode within view of the main war party. Naim broke rank at the head of the column and galloped back. Reaching them, he reined his horse in and spun it around beside them. At a nod from Wayth, he shouted a command and the riders spurred their horses to a canter.

XVII THE DOOR

COLYN was overwhelmed by the size of the army. It flowed out before him like a river in a swirling, bobbing mass of men, women and horses.

"How many soldiers are there?" he asked.

"We are three thousand and eighty," Wayth said.

"So many!" Colyn said.

Wayth looked at the boy and smiled sadly. "No, Rykone," he said. "So few. Not so long ago this would have been merely the vanguard of our army. Now it is the body."

The Kinroan ahead seemed to have stopped. Seeing Wayth and Naim's party approaching, several riders broke away from the main company and galloped towards them. They rode at breakneck speed, spears pointed, yelling. Several from Wayth's party also broke rank, lowered their spears and charged. Just as it seemed that the riders were going to run each other through, they swerved to the side and reined their horses in, whooping and laughing.

The three warriors from the main company rode on to speak with Wayth and Naim.

"We survived," Wayth said in answer to their questions. "But it is a long story. There's no time to tell it now."

He spurred his horse to a gallop, whacking the rump of Colyn's mare at the same time so that she started to gallop too. Naim followed suit, but Insay remained behind.

"A tale for the fireside!" Wayth called back as he raced towards the main war party.

The warriors in front made way for Wayth, Colyn and Naim, and the three rode on unhindered except for the constant calls of greeting. Colyn suddenly realised that they were not too far from their destination. About half a kilometre ahead of the foremost rider, he could see the right-angled bend in the valley around which the great waterfall was hidden.

They trotted on through the stationary column until they came in sight of several men lifting and tying something behind a team of waiting horses. The two men and the boy reined in their own mounts and looked on.

"That's it!" Colyn said, leaning in the saddle to peer past his mare's neck. As he leaned he began to slip. He clutched at her mane.

"Steady!" Wayth said, catching him and pushing him upright. "You'll have to wait until your feet reach the stirrups before you can lean out like that."

"But that's the door!" Colyn said, straightening himself up.

Wayth laughed. "Yes, Rykone. That's the door."

Colyn peered as best he could past the mare's tossing head. The triangle of cardboard he had cut from the box in his father's shed lay on the ground. Kinzar trotted around it, sniffing, as two men levered one corner off the ground with an iron bar and another looped some rope under it.

"What are they doing?" Colyn asked.

"They're just settling it on a new litter," Naim said. "The poles wear out quickly as we drag it along."

"But why don't they just carry it?" Colyn asked.

The two men looked at him strangely but did not answer. They dismounted and Wayth lifted Colyn down.

Colyn ran over to the men by the litter. "Why don't you carry it?" he said, picking the door up by one corner.

The man with the rope let it fall from his hands. The other two men dropped the bar they had been using for a lever. They stood gaping at the boy.

Wayth, trying to hide his shock, said, "This is the Knife Lord."

The three men stiffened to attention and bowed their heads.

News of Colyn's feat spread through the company. Men and women came racing on horse and on foot to see the boy who was stronger than ten men. More warriors arrived and more still. They stood looking at him, some with horses tugging at the reins in their hands, others with hands empty.

A man close to Colyn withdrew his dagger from its sheath. He turned the weapon to hold it by its blade, crooked his left arm in front of himself, and rested the dagger-handle on his forearm. Others followed his example, until the whole company stood looking at Colyn, dagger-blades pointing at their own chests and handles pointing at Colyn.

Colyn looked at Wayth, confused.

Wayth cleared his throat. "They are offering you their blades, their hearts," he said.

Colyn looked at the warriors slowly, turning around to see the complete circle of faces. Then he did something that he had not planned and about which he could barely guess the significance. Letting the door lean against his leg, he withdrew his own knife from his belt and, holding it by the blade, he rested it on his left forearm and offered it to the Kinroan.

A murmur ran through the horde of warriors, then there was silence. Wayth said something to them—a single word that Colyn did not catch. They sheathed their daggers and turned to go about their business.

"This once I wish I were from your world," Wayth said, touching the door. "Lay it down."

Colyn let it fall. It hit the ground with a thud, like a concrete slab, sending up a puff of dust. Wayth wedged his fingers underneath it and tried to lift it but could not. He looked at Colyn, who picked it up with one hand, holding it by one corner between forefinger and thumb.

"Perhaps he could carry it on the back of the mare," Naim said. "We could travel much faster."

Wayth looked at the boy and then at the horse. "Could you do it, Rykone?" he asked.

"Yes," Colyn said, "if you help me up."

Wayth stooped to hoist Colyn into the saddle but could not lift him. He sat down with a grunt.

"It's the door," he said. "I can't lift you while you're holding it."

"You could lift me up then pass it to me," Colyn said.

"No," Wayth said. "Ten of us couldn't lift the door that high."

"Could you climb on to those rocks and then on to the horse's back, Rykone?" Naim asked. He pointed to a rocky outcrop a few metres away.

"Easy," said Colyn, and set off.

Wayth led the mare over while Colyn climbed the rocks. When she was in position, he scrambled on to her back, holding the cardboard triangle.

The great horse swayed. She neighed in fear. Her front legs began to wobble. Wayth called out in alarm and stepped back. Kinzar barked furiously.

"Throw the door!" Naim cried. "Quick! The door!"

Colyn threw the door to one side as the horse began to collapse. She fell forward, crashing to her knees, as the door smashed to the ground, narrowly missing Wayth. Colyn knotted his fingers in the mare's mane to keep himself from falling as she steadied herself and struggled to stand again.

Naim ran to the mare and inspected her front legs. He ran his hand up and down each leg, then slapped the big muscles on her chest. "Good girl!" he said. "You'll be all right. Good girl."

Wayth patted Colyn's leg. "Well," he said, "either we rope and drag it again or you carry it on foot."

Colyn looked towards the bend in the valley. "It's not far," he said, slipping down from his mount. "I'll carry it."

He picked up the door and set off. Wayth and Naim walked beside him, leading their stallions.

"A boy with a door to two worlds," Naim said, shaking his head in amazement. "And look how lightly he carries it!"

To hide his pride and embarrassment, Colyn asked, "How did you get the door?"

"Three days ago," Wayth replied, "our watchmen saw a dragon flying with it at dusk towards the Mountain Lairs. The beast was flying slowly, and low to the ground, because of its burden. Our men shot and killed it. That is how we came by the door, Rykone."

XVIII THE BATTLE

A CRY went out, first from one voice, then from many. Colyn looked to where the whole army was now gazing. The dragons were coming, flying up the valley from the direction of the sea. They looked like crows, tiny with distance.

Instantly every warrior was on the move. To Colyn the scene seemed to be one of utter confusion. Shouts rang out. Horses neighed and pranced. Warriors ran towards each other or swung into their saddles.

Within a minute, however, Colyn could see that the movement was not random but orderly. Already fifty or sixty warriors stood in two rows behind the army, facing the approaching dragons. They stood in perfect formation about four metres apart, whirling their slings, limbering up and waiting for the dragons to come within range. They moved like dancers, their upper bodies swaying with the sweep of their arms and the weight of the stones in their pouches.

Archers, most of them women, had positioned themselves behind the slingmen. They stood in closer formation, bows strung, arrows at the ready. Insay was among them.

Behind them the spearmen stood, their spears butted in the soil, waiting to impale any low-flying dragon that had been wounded by the missiles from the front ranks. They stood so closely together that they looked like a single giant porcupine.

Warriors with crossbows scrambled up the valley sides, searching for positions.

Wayth galloped towards the slingmen and gave them the stones Colyn had made with his knife.

Mounted warriors closed about Colyn, blocking his view of the defensive formations. Somehow Wayth made his way back through the throng to his side. But Naim had gone.

"Well," Wayth said, almost happily, "can you run, Rykone?"

Colyn nodded. He tucked the door under his arm and began to run. The riders—perhaps a third of the Kinroan army—began to move with him: a thousand mounted warriors surrounding a single boy, trotting towards the valley's bend, travelling at the pace of the boy's running.

By the time they had covered a quarter of a kilometre, which was half the distance to the valley bend, the dragons had reached the Kinroan formation.

As the first dragons came in range, the first rank of slingmen slung their stones—the stones Colyn had made. Some whistled past their targets, but most struck home. It was a massacre. The potato-stones exploded on impact, killing or crippling every dragon they hit. Some beasts fell to the ground at the slingmen's feet. Others smashed into the valley walls. Still others flapped away wounded.

The cheers of the Kinroan were drowned by the screams of the dragons. The few beasts who were unwounded veered away, out of range. But the second formation came on.

The slingmen slung their missiles again. But this time they only had ordinary stones. All the potato-stones had been used in the first counter-attack. The stones bounced off the thick scales without doing much damage but they were effective enough to break the formation. The dragons swerved away and flapped higher to safety. Several had holes in their wings.

One dragon was struck by a stone on the wing bone and began to wobble dangerously. The archers focused their attention on it. Many arrows struck its scales and bounced off. Several arrows pierced the soft places in the creases around the dragon's legs and wings. The beast began to lose height. The slingmen rained stones on it again, battering its weakened body. The dragon fell, landing at the feet of the slingmen, who drew their daggers and killed it.

The dragons roared with rage. Twenty of them began to dive on the Kinroan at once. The slingmen hurled their stones. Still the dragons came. The archers fired. One dragon was struck in the eye and flew off, screaming. But the others kept coming. As they drew closer they began to breathe fire. Flame flared from their nostrils in great orange bursts.

The warriors held up their shields for protection, but many of them were too slow and the spouting flames seared them. The orderly ranks broke up as men and women ran into each other in pain and panic.

The dragons veered away and re-grouped. Swooping again, they killed many more warriors with their fire.

One dragon managed to snatch a woman in its talons. The crossbow warriors filled its body with armour-piercing iron quarrels, and it fell, dead as the Kinroan it held.

Another dragon, flying low, received several spears in its underbelly. It crashed into the warriors who were riding with Colyn, killing a dozen riders and their horses as it skidded along the ground.

The riders turned to fight. Colyn dodged his way between the horses and suddenly found himself alone in front of the army.

A huge dragon spotted him and began to dive towards him. It folded its wings and hurtled down like a giant spear. Colyn knelt, using the door as a shield. The dragon breathed out fire. The flame struck the cardboard shield and fanned out. Colyn crouched unharmed. The dragon kept coming, spouting fire, until it seemed it would actually hit the shield. But moments before impact, the beast swung upwards. Colyn leaped to his feet and thrust his knife up with both hands. The blade sank into the dragon's throat. There was a gurgling sound and hot blood gushed down on to him. The dragon was gliding too quickly to stop. It sped on and Colyn held the knife up all the while so that it sliced along the dragon's throat and belly and tail, opening it up from end to end. The beast was dead before it hit the ground.

Colyn was covered in sticky black blood. It steamed

and stank on him, but he did not have time to worry about it. He picked up the door and dashed around the bend in the valley. Kinzar raced with him.

The enormous falls jumped into sight. He ran towards them, noticing with relief that warriors with crossbows were in position above and below the falls. His lungs felt as if they were going to burn up, but he kept running.

Hoof-beats sounded behind him, and he looked back over his shoulder to see Wayth gaining on him. He reached the falls and stopped.

Wayth swung out of his saddle while his horse was still moving. Both horse and rider nearly skidded into the falls. He turned to look back at the valley's bend. No one followed.

Wayth knelt before Colyn. "Go quickly, Rykone!" he said.

"But what about you?" Colyn said, breathing hard. "I could help."

"You will help by sealing the entrance," Wayth said.

"But there is so much I want to know," Colyn said. "About me and Kinzar and you."

"There is no time," Wayth said, rising to his feet. "But I will tell you one thing: you will find some answers in the puzzle. Complete the puzzle with your father. You should be together when you learn the truth."

Wayth looked at the sky at the valley's bend. "You must go," he said. "You must seal the door. We cannot hold the dragons long. The falls are too wide and high. Some will get through."

Colyn had tears in his eyes. "Will I ever see you again?"

Wayth smiled sadly. "You have the knife. And Kinzar.

They will bring you back. Perhaps I will live till then."

Several riders galloped around the bend.

Wayth hugged Colyn tightly, then pushed him away. "Go quickly," he said. "Two worlds wait on you."

The riders dismounted swiftly and took up positions beside Wayth, their bows at the ready, their horses pawing the dust beside them.

Another rider galloped around the bend. Colyn was pleased to see it was Naim, then horrified to see two dragons in hot pursuit. Sensing that the beasts were too close, Naim swung his horse around and lifted his shield. The first dragon lashed the shield from his arm with its tail, and the second swooped in to burn him.

"No!" Colyn screamed. "No!"

In a blind fury he thrust his knife through his belt and plunged his hand into his pocket. He withdrew two stones and hurled them with all his might, one after the other, at the first dragon. They both sped from his hand and exploded on target like rockets. The dragon swerved wildly to the right, struck the valley wall, then crashed to the ground. The second dragon fled.

Colyn began to run towards Naim, but Wayth caught him.

"Go," he said. "Make his death count. Keep the dragons out of Nalkrist."

Colyn was shaking. Without a word he turned. Holding the door tightly under his arm, he plunged through the waterfall. Kinzar followed him, and found him in the mists.

STILL holding Kinzar's tail, Colyn stepped from the thick mists into the clean, clear air of his father's shed. He was pale and shaken from his ordeal, and close to panic. He let go of his dog's tail and juggled the cardboard triangle through the hole in the box.

When he looked up, he jumped with fright and reached for his knife.

Two men were standing by the box, one on either side of the entrance. They were both well armed, with leather armour, brass helmets, shields, spears, daggers and swords. One had a bow and quiver slung across his shoulders while the other had a sling and pebble-pouch tucked in his belt.

Colyn pointed his knife first at one and then at the other.

The men looked at the knife, then at him. "Rykone," they said, bowing.

"Who are you?" Colyn asked, his heart racing.

"We are Kinroan," one man said, taking a step forward. "We were lost, but Kinzar found us."

"Oh!" Colyn exclaimed. "You! The sons of Ekome!"

The men grinned. Their teeth were very white in their tanned faces. "You know us?" The same man, the smaller and younger of the two, spoke again.

"Yes. We sent Kinzar after you. But he came back alone so we thought you were lost forever."

"No," the younger one said. "Kinzar brought us here. We have been guarding the doorway."

"Not that we needed to." The other brother spoke for the first time. "We've seen neither fang nor scale of a dragon."

"Boy!" Colyn said. "Wayth will be glad!"

"How is Wayth?" asked the younger man eagerly. "And the others?"

"You have the door," the other man remarked. "Was there a battle?"

At the mention of the door, Colyn remembered what he was supposed to do. "Yes, there is a battle," he said. "Wayth and the others are holding the dragons at the falls. Naim is dead and I have to close the doorway. That's the only way I can make his death count." He lifted the door to put it in place. "Quick! Wayth said to be quick!"

The younger brother raised his hand. "But Rykone," he said, "we must go back."

Colyn looked at him, pondering what to do, then laid the door aside.

"Sit, Kinzar," he said, pointing to the door. The dog sat obediently on the piece of cardboard. "I'll just be a minute, boy," he said. "Bark to bring me back."

"I can only get you on to the beach," Colyn told the brothers. "It's a long walk to the hills."

He started to step through the doorway, then stopped. "You must be hungry," he said. He ran to a sack of potatoes, grabbed a handful, and handed them to the two men. "They taste better cooked but you can eat them raw." He reached into his pockets for the potato-stones he had left. "Here," he said. "If the dragons attack you, throw these. They go really fast."

Colyn stepped through the doorway and the Kinroan followed after. He cut a doorway in the mists and heard them gasp as the otherworld came into sight.

The two men stepped through the doorway and turned to say farewell. Colyn could see them clearly, and the shock on their faces when they realised that the doorway he had cut in the mists was not visible from their world. He reached out to them and they took his hand and kissed it.

Kinzar began to bark. Colyn turned from Klarin and ran for home.

In the shed he snatched a roll of masking tape from the workbench and tore a strip off. He slotted the door into place and stuck the tape over one of the cracks, then tore off another length of tape and sealed the second crack.

Kinzar began to bark furiously as Colyn tore off a third length. He looked, and to his horror he saw a glint of yellow through the bottom crack. He cried out and in his panic he tangled the length of masking tape. He fumbled with the roll, trying to lift the edge with his nail to start the next strip. The dragon roared and snorted. Orange flames shot out along the bottom of the door. Colyn fell back, holding his hands to his face to stop the heat. More flames shot out and the box began to burn. Colyn watched, terrified that at any moment a dragon would leap out of the flames. He sat fixed to the spot, watching the box burn.

"Colyn! Colyn!" his father called, running into the shed. "What on earth is going on! Do you want to burn the place down?"

He grabbed a hessian sack and began to beat the flames. He lashed at them until nothing but smouldering ash remained. Then he turned to look at his son in disbelief.

"Boy," he said, his voice shaking with anger. "Boy, I ... " His voice faltered.

Colyn was staring at the ashes. Tears were rolling down his cheeks.

His father came and sat down beside him. "Son," he said, "I don't know what's got into you lately." He put his arms around Colyn and hugged him. Colyn leaned into him heavily. He sobbed and sobbed while his father hugged him tightly. "I haven't the foggiest," he said.

SITTING in the sunlight in the doorway of the packing shed, his father and his dog on either side of him, Colyn recounted everything.

His father listened silently and seriously. He never once interrupted, although he often rested his hand on Colyn's shoulder or squeezed his arm.

At last Colyn had no more to tell. He looked into his father's face, and his father looked away towards the river. Colyn gazed towards the river gums too. Kinzar laid his head in Colyn's lap. A crow cawed in the distance, breaking the silence beautifully.

"Perhaps all this would have happened to me if I hadn't lost the knife when I was a boy," his father said at last. He hugged Colyn tightly and sighed. "Who knows? Right now I don't know anything."

They held on to each other for a long time.

"So," his father said, letting Colyn go. "That bloke said we should finish the puzzle?"

Colyn nodded. "Wayth. He said the puzzle has the answers. Or some of them, anyway."

His father stood up and stretched. "Well," he said,

"let's go into the house and finish it." He looked at Colyn. "But first you had better have a shower and wash off that dragon's blood."

For the first time Colyn noticed the blood, and the smell. Some of it had washed off when he stepped through the waterfall, but it still caked his clothes and smeared his skin.

While Colyn was in the shower, his father made him an omelette and a mug of hot chocolate. The boy looked much better once he was washed and dressed in clean clothes. He looked better still after he had eaten.

"Now for the puzzle," his father said as he took the dirty plate to the sink.

With his first glance at the puzzle, Colyn gasped. "The rider!" he said.

"Yes, I finished him while you slept last night. He's magnificent, isn't he?"

The warrior on the rearing stallion was holding his shield above his head to ward off the dragon's flames. His head was turned down and slightly to the left, as if he were looking for something on the ground just outside the picture. His long black hair was blown about, like the horse's mane and tail. His face was without fear or hate. It showed courage and resignation, and was deeply handsome.

"That's Wayth!" Colyn said.

"The one who came for you?"

Colyn nodded.

His father thought for a moment. "And that is like the dragons you fought?" he said, pointing to the beast in the puzzle.

"Exactly the same," Colyn said.

"This is pretty weird, son. How could we have a puzzle picturing real people and real creatures—and maybe even real events—from another world?"

Before Colyn could reply, his father said, "Well, let's see what other surprises we can piece together."

They worked without speaking for some time. They concentrated on the right-hand side, extending out from Wayth and the dragon. Gradually more riders and dragons came into view. Men on foot brandished swords and spears, or fired arrows and stones. Broken weapons and dying warriors lay on the ground, along with dead and dying dragons and horses.

"It must have been a terrible battle," Colyn's father said.

"It was," Colyn said. "The Kinroan lost most of their warriors that day."

His father looked at him strangely. "How do you know?" he said.

"Wayth and Insay told me. This must be the battle they were talking about."

Colyn pressed the last piece of a warrior's face into position. "That man is Naim," he said. He was not particularly surprised by this discovery. In fact, after seeing Wayth in the picture, he rather expected to find Naim.

"The one who died?"

"Yes," Colyn said, determined not to cry.

And still they worked, sorting through the pieces, trying the same piece in different places before searching for another that would fit. It was growing dark. Colyn turned the light on.

"Do you think we'll finish it tonight?" Colyn asked.

"At the rate we're going, perhaps," his father said. "I told you it took your mother and me two weeks to do this puzzle, didn't I?"

"Yes," Colyn said. "But you probably didn't work on it hard."

"No, I suppose not," his father said. "Your mother could have done it herself, while I was in the paddocks, but she said we should do it together. And when we worked on it at night she was either tired or dreamy. Pregnant women are like that."

Colyn found that doing the puzzle was like carving wood: it went better if he did not think too hard about it.

"Dad," he asked, "why did you spell my name with a 'y' instead of an 'i'? Most people spell my name 'C-o-l-i-n'."

"I thought I told you," his father said without looking up. "In fact, I'm sure I have. You must've forgotten ..." Then the puzzle made *him* forget. "Look at that," he said. "It's a woman's leg."

Colyn looked at the leg in the stirrup of the half-finished horse his father was working on. "Yes," he said. "But why did you put a 'y' in my name?"

"My name is Con," his father said. "And your mother's name was Lyn, so we joined the two together. You got half of mine and all of hers."

"So my name contains her name," Colyn said thoughtfully. Then he brightened up. "Actually," he said, "if you drop out the 'l' and the 'y', I've got all of your name, too."

"Ha, so you have!" His father was pleased. "Why didn't I see that before?"

But it was the puzzle that had his attention. "Look for pieces of the woman," he said. "Let's try to finish her before we have tea."

There were not many pieces left, so it was not too difficult to find the ones that made up the woman.

She was mounted on a steely-grey mare and wore Kinroan armour. Her hair was auburn and her skin was fair. Her face was beautiful but frightened. She was looking up at a place in the puzzle that had not yet been pieced together. Both Colyn and his father knew what was waiting in that patch of unfinished sky.

"She's holding up my knife," Colyn said.

His father had gone quite pale. He turned from the table and left the room. Colyn heard him go into his bedroom and rummage about. After a while he returned with a photograph, which he laid on the table beside the picture of the woman.

"It's my mother," Colyn said with sudden recognition.

"It's my wife," his father said. "My darling." He stared in bewilderment. "How can it be? I would have recognised her when I first did the puzzle. But I don't even remember a woman in it when we did it together. How can it be?"

Colyn had no answers, only questions. "How did she die?" he asked.

His father shook his head.

"Tell me, Dad. Please. I'm old enough now."

His father struggled to find words to say what he did not like even to think. "I found her body by the river at the edge of the potato paddock after a thunderstorm," he said at last. "She was badly burned, and I thought she had been struck by lightning."

"It was the dragons," Colyn said. "She was the Rykona, and they killed her."

"Yes," his father said. "The dragons." And he began to weep. A mighty weeping, like a broken dam.

Colyn wept too. In this way they comforted each other.

When they had no more tears, Colyn said, "I'm going to go back and kill those dragons."

"No, son," his father said. "You'll need a better reason than hate to go back."

Colyn was quiet for a moment. He turned his knife over in his hand, studying it. How beautiful it was, and how magical! He had owned it for barely two weeks but already it had changed his life forever. "Well anyway," he said finally, "one day I *will* go back, with Kinzar, and with my knife."

ABOUT THE AUTHOR

ANDREW LANSDOWN is the author of several books and has been a contributor to a number of poetry and short fiction anthologies. His work is published regularly in literary journals and newspapers.

Mr. Lansdown lives in Boyup Brook, Western Australia, with his wife and three children.